Deep in the Heart of HIGH SCHOOL

Deep in the Heart of HIGH SCHOOL

Veronica Goldbach

Farrar Straus Giroux • New York

www.fsgkidsbooks.com

Library of Congress Cataloging-in-Publication Data
Goldbach, Veronica.
    Deep in the heart of high school / Veronica Goldbach.— 1st ed.
        p.   cm.
    Summary: Three friends, Olivia Silverstein, Fatima Garcia, and Vanessa
Reynolds, help one another through family troubles, romantic crushes, and the
perils of freshman year at a San Antonio, Texas, high school.
    ISBN-13: 978-0-374-32330-1
    ISBN-10: 0-374-32330-5
    [1. Best friends—Fiction.   2. Friendship—Fiction.   3. High schools—Fiction.
4. Schools—Fiction.   5. Family life—Texas—Fiction.   6. San Antonio (Tex.)—
Fiction.]   I. Title.

PZ7.G56373 Dee 2009
[Fic]—dc22

                                                                2008000814

For Elaine Goldbach, the Dream Crusher—
this was all your idea

Deep in the Heart of HIGH SCHOOL

PROLOGUE

Olivia Silverstein stared out the car window. Her mother had dragged them to the cemetery to "celebrate" her father's birthday. It was a morbid thing to do. Talk about how old he would have been. Toss some flowers on the ground. Pray, cry, feel uncomfortable, and clean the headstone.

Rosa, Olivia's twelve-year-old sister, sat in the front seat, the air-conditioning vents pointed her way. At the graveyard, Rosa hadn't gotten her hands dirty. She had barely left the car.

Olivia had worked twice as hard using Q-tips to clean the dirt between the letters in her father's name. She did it to make her mom happy. Mrs. Silverstein seemed to think these visits were important. But Olivia thought it was less painful to live without a father than to go stare at a grave and be reminded of his death every holiday.

Mrs. Silverstein seemed totally unaware of Olivia's troubles. She hummed along to the radio, tapping the steering wheel as she drove. Olivia and her mother had tried to maintain a conversation, but had given up when the only thing Rosa would do was complain about the heat.

After her father died, Olivia had decided she should try to make life easier for her mother. She'd heard that a person gets used to loss. That eventually life gets back to normal. Her father died almost two years ago. When, Olivia wondered, would things get better? When would she get to have her own life?

Fatima Garcia dragged a heavy branch across the lawn. Her parents had had laborers, not children. She tossed the branch onto a growing pile in front of the house. Then she walked back up the driveway to watch her father swing from tree to tree with a chain saw. His only protection was a rope tied around his waist. No gloves or helmet. Only a rope and her uncle shouting directions.

The sight would have made Fatima nervous if she hadn't seen her father do his Tarzan routine hundreds of times before. Her father swung from trees, balanced on steep rooftops, crawled under houses, roasted in poorly ventilated attics, did anything his brother's construction business required of him, without hesitation.

The lady whose trees they were cutting stood wringing her hands. Fatima could tell she'd never hire them again.

When she'd asked for tree trimmers, she probably hadn't expected two men, an overweight woman, and a truck full of Mexican kids to show up. Small children running under a man balanced on a branch using a chain saw had given the poor woman heart palpitations, so Mrs. Garcia had taken Fatima's sister and brothers home. Fatima was the only hauler left. This job was going to take hours, she thought, pushing her glasses up on the bridge of her nose. Her constant sweating kept causing them to slip.

Fatima wanted to be done. She felt awful. She was wearing a stained T-shirt and her most torn-up jeans, parading her fat self up and down this lady's perfect lawn on the good side of town where no one liked to see wetback laborers. She had helped her father on jobs for as long as she could remember. When, she wondered, would she get used to being an embarrassment?

Vanessa Reynolds opened yet another black trash bag filled with her belongings. Moving was supposed to be exciting, not excruciating. She had been in San Antonio a few months and she hated it. She had lived in an actual house back in Plano, a wealthy suburb of Dallas. A house with walk-in closets, a laundry room, and a pool. Now all she had was a stagnant pond, a tiny two-bedroom apartment, and a coin-operated washer and dryer in the basement. Vanna supposed she should be grateful that they had finally found a place. No more sleeping on her mother's friends'

couches. But back home she'd been someone important, complete with a ton of friends and a hot boyfriend. High school should have been the best time of her life. Instead, Vanna had to start over as a nobody at a new school and that hot boyfriend hadn't called once since she moved. She didn't want to think about what that meant.

Vanna crammed more clothes into her pitifully small closet. Focus on the good, she told herself. She had two friends, Fatima and Olivia. She'd met them during freshman band camp back in August. They'd bonded over the heat and evil section leaders. Vanna already felt like she'd known them for years.

Vanna would get used to her "new" life. She had to. There was no way she ever wanted her parents to get back together. No way she ever wanted to see her father again.

Still, she wondered, how long would it take for her to adjust? To feel normal? Another week? A month? Maybe forever.

1

Fatima Garcia had been in school band since sixth grade, and she had only recently figured something out. Something no one tells you when you sign up and pick your instrument. After just about two months as a member of the Alexander Hamilton High School marching band, Fatima finally understood the social hierarchy of band.

At the top of the food chain was the drumline. They rivaled football players in high school popularity. They had none of the geekiness usually associated with band members. No gross spit valves on their instruments. They were never red-faced or light-headed from lack of oxygen, like the brass or woodwinds. No, they were simply cool. Drummers had to be confident. They kept the beat. They were in control and they knew it. They did their thing and didn't care what anyone thought.

Next came the low brass: tubas, baritones, and trombones. Big, manly instruments usually played by big, manly guys and the occasional tough girl. They were the bass of the band, what gave the band the thumping, like living subwoofers. Strong from carrying huge instruments, they were a group nobody messed with. Not even football players.

Trumpets followed. Trumpets were the section that carried the melody. The show-offs of the band. Big talkers, but not nearly as tough as the low brass. A few nerds filtered into this section.

Female flutes were the coolest of the woodwinds. Like their instruments, they tended to be thin and twitter in high-pitched, breathy voices. Flutes didn't often get to carry the melody. They were more the cheerleaders of the band, playing harmony or background.

Clarinets ranked right below flutes. Not nearly as girlie as the flutes, clarinets did the grunt work of the band. They backed up the trumpets on melody, beefed up the bass line with the low brass, and helped the flutes with trills and runs.

French horns were near the bottom, barely above oboes and male flutes. Saxophones were the wild card. They could be as cool as trumpets with their smooth jazziness or as nerdy as oboes with their random squeaks. Mostly, they moved easily throughout the groups, blending in well.

Fatima and her friends simply had the misfortune of being matched up with the wrong instruments. Olivia, Fatima's best friend since kindergarten, was tall and thin with very long brown hair. She was delicate-looking, like a flute, but had the people-pleasing personality of a clarinet. Olivia, however, played saxophone.

Fatima's newest friend, Vanna, had been in San Antonio only a few months, but it was easy to see she did not belong with her section. Vanna played trombone. With her perfect body, gorgeously curly red hair, huge blue eyes, and flirtatious nature, she would have made the perfect flute.

Alex Menchaca, Fatima's off-and-on friend since first grade, rounded out their little misfit group. Alex had the mouth of a trumpet and the odd sense of humor of a saxophone. But he played French horn.

As for Fatima, she had the bulk of a tuba player and the cynicism of a drummer. Back in sixth grade she had stupidly picked out flute as her instrument. Big mistake. The other flute players went out of their way to avoid her. They made it seem like Fatima's fatness was contagious. She actually enjoyed playing the flute and she was pretty good at it.

The band hierarchy was never more obvious than when bands gathered for competitions. Fatima saw it reflected in every band gathered outside San Antonio's Alamodome on the first weekend in October. The uniforms may have been different, but the division was the same.

Fatima and her friends were crowded into a small shady spot. A shady but by no means cool spot. As usual they were talking about Travis Martinez. Travis was a sophomore trumpet player and the love of Olivia's life, only he didn't know it.

"What kind of stalker are you if you won't even stand near him?" Vanna demanded.

"I'm not a stalker," Olivia replied. As much as she tried not to, she couldn't helping looking at Travis. The sun was shining on his sandy brown hair. His broad shoulders filled out his white uniform jacket quite nicely. He was tall and solid. When Olivia was around him, she turned into a zombie, unable to talk or think.

"She'd probably have to talk to him to be considered a stalker," Fatima agreed.

"True," Vanna said. "There's a group of French horns next to Travis. Maybe Alex could go talk to them."

"Why would I do that?" Alex asked.

"They're your people. We'll all go over there with you and Olivia can strike up a conversation with Travis," Vanna suggested.

As much as they explained it, Vanna didn't really get the whole Travis/Olivia saga. It had been going on since seventh grade. Olivia would never talk to Travis. Fatima and Alex had accepted that long ago. Vanna, however, seemed determined to push. And Olivia, as quiet as she was, could be pretty stubborn.

Now both Fatima and Alex shook their heads.

Olivia didn't move. The idea of casual conversation with Travis filled her with anxiety. What, she wondered, was wrong with her? Why couldn't she just talk to him like a normal person?

But there wasn't time anyway, as the drum major called

the band to attention. What followed was an impassioned pep talk. Most of the speech focused on how Last Stand at the Alamodome was one of the few contests where Hamilton High was able to face bands from the wealthy northside schools. Usually HHS competed against other inner-city schools. This was their chance to show everyone they were just as good as those rich kids. Even if their school couldn't afford special effects for their show or private tutors. Or to clean the uniforms more than twice a year, Vanna added silently. She was only half listening. The band would show everyone, blah, blah, blah.

Vanna was annoyed with Olivia for passing up another opportunity to talk to Travis. How could Olivia claim to be in love with Travis and not want to talk to him? It didn't make any sense. But, then again, what did Vanna know about love?

The drum major finished and the band took the field with the low brass blasting the bass line of Daddy Yankee's "Gasolina," a song that never failed to get the crowd on its feet. This was when putting up with all the icky stuff that came along with marching band was worth it. The stupid band camp jokes, the hours of practicing, and the countless push-ups were forgotten.

"Gasolina" led into the drum break, the drumline's big moment. The rest of the band danced. The crowd went nuts. The moves might have looked raunchy and improvised, but they had been practiced to uniform precision.

The drum break led into a medley of Selena songs.

Vanna didn't know much about Selena Quintanilla-Pérez other than that Jennifer Lopez had been in a movie about the singer's life. In San Antonio, the slain Tejano singer had almost godlike status. The crowd stopped screaming and began singing along. Vanna could play the songs "Amor Prohibido," "Bidi Bidi Bom Bom," and "Como La Flor," but she couldn't sing the lyrics. She was totally clueless about Spanish, the unofficial language of San Antonio.

The crowd roared when the show ended. Vanna basked in the taste of rock stardom for a few seconds before the band marched off. In the midst of all the frenzy, Vanna couldn't help remembering that in that huge crowd there was one person missing: Claire Reynolds, Vanna's mother.

2

"Chop up those potatoes. I think we better use them before they go bad," Mrs. Silverstein said. Olivia was helping her mother make their usual Saturday night dinner: *mingongo*. Olivia didn't know if *mingongo* was an actual Spanish word. Fatima, who spoke fluent Spanish, had never heard of it. The idea was to use up whatever vegetables they had before going grocery shopping on Sunday.

"Fourth place is really good," Olivia's mom added.

"No one from our district has ever made it in the top ten before. Mr. Mendez was really proud." Olivia was disappointed. She'd thought they had marched their best show ever.

"Are you sure we can use these potatoes?" Olivia asked. There were sprouty things growing out of them.

Mrs. Silverstein glanced at them. "Sure, just cut that stuff off."

Olivia's mom never wasted food. She said it came from growing up poor with six brothers. She could stretch pretty much anything into a meal as long as she had rice or potatoes or eggs. And it didn't matter if the eggs were expired. To her, expiration dates were more like suggestions. She always reasoned that if she cooked something long enough it would be okay. No one had been poisoned yet. Olivia found a can of peas and carrots and handed it to her mother.

"Y'all looked amazing," Mrs. Silverstein praised.

"I can't believe they let you guys dance like that," Rosa said, wandering into the kitchen. "We'd get in big trouble if we tried those moves on our dance team."

"Band's different. It's impossible to look too suggestive in our uniforms," Olivia explained.

"I should have stayed in band," Rosa mumbled. She stood on her tiptoes and flipped channels on the small white television that sat on top of the refrigerator. Rosa had been in band for a week before she decided she wasn't cut out for it. Her flute now sat gathering dust in the attic somewhere.

"I'm going to start back at the jewelry store next week," Mrs. Silverstein announced.

Both girls groaned. After Olivia's dad died, Mrs. Silverstein found that her teaching salary was not enough to support them. Every once in a while she would pick up shifts at a jewelry store in the mall. This meant she would almost never be home, and when she was she was either exhausted or in a bad mood. It also meant Olivia would have to take over the cooking, cleaning, dog walking, and helping Rosa with homework.

"I know. I hate it, too," Mrs. Silverstein said in response to the groaning. "But we really need the money. I've got to get the heater fixed before winter, and it can't hurt to start saving for Christmas."

Peanut, Olivia's black-and-white terrihuahua, whined at her feet.

"Olivia, why don't you take the dogs for a walk while Rosa and I finish up here," Mrs. Silverstein suggested.

Rosa was engrossed in watching *Wuthering Heights*, one of her absolute favorites. If that was on, she wouldn't be doing anything for a while. Olivia would probably end up helping her mom set the table and warm tortillas after the dog walk.

Olivia sighed and leashed up Peanut and the two other family dogs. As they dragged her down the block, Olivia found herself daydreaming about Travis Martinez asking her out. But who was she kidding. She was too tall, too skinny, and had too frizzy hair for him to notice her in that way.

"So," Vanna was telling her mom about the day's contest, "right before they announced the winners all the bands took the field in one big group and had to play 'Texas, Our Texas,' 'Deep in the Heart of Texas,' and 'The Eyes of Texas,' which sounds exactly like 'I've Been Working on the

Railroad.' Cheesy, huh? I'm surprised they didn't have some Alamo song for us to play." It seemed like everywhere Vanna looked in San Antonio there was some picture or reference to the Alamo, the mission church where Davy Crockett and other Texans waged their last stand for Texas's independence from Mexico. They were killed by the Mexican army. But "Remember the Alamo!" became the battle cry of the revolution. The Alamo was the city's claim to fame. Vanna got that, but did every business have to be called Alamo something or other? Alamo Bakery, Alamo Car Repair, Alamo Dry Cleaning, Alamo Pest Control, and so on.

"I can only imagine," Mrs. Reynolds said.

"I guess you'd have to," Vanna mumbled, but her mother didn't seem to notice. What a surprise.

Vanna and her mom sat on the couch watching TV and eating Chinese/Mexican food from Vanna's favorite restaurant, China Latina. Her mother had bought it to try to make up for not going to the contest.

"Dahlia and I are going out in a little while," Vanna's mother said during the commercial break.

"So, now you have energy," Vanna snapped. What happened to being too exhausted to go to the band contest?

"Don't start," Mrs. Reynolds said tiredly. "You know I really need her support right now."

Vanna shrugged. They had moved to San Antonio so her mom could be closer to her best friend. She and Dahlia had known each other since they were in high school. So, when Claire Reynolds had decided she couldn't live in the same city as her ex-husband, she and Vanna had moved in with Dahlia. No one seemed to care that Vanna's life had been totally destroyed.

"Why don't you go out with one of your friends from band tonight?" her mother offered. "It might make you feel better."

Vanna ignored her mother and took the trash to the kitchen. Her mother was beautiful. Her blond hair was always perfectly arranged and her clothes always complemented her figure, but she was a secret slob. If Vanna waited until her mother felt like cleaning up, there'd be mold on the take-out boxes.

As Vanna walked back into the living room, the phone rang. She didn't bother answering it. Hardly anyone ever called her. Every once in a while her old friends from Plano or Olivia or Fatima would call, but that was it. Her boyfriend, Troy, still hadn't found the time to return her calls.

Her mother picked up the phone, mumbled a few words, and walked into her bedroom. What did she need privacy for?

Vanna muted the volume on the TV so she could try to overhear whom her mother was talking to. Before her parents split up, Vanna and her mom had been good friends. They didn't have secrets.

"Well, rent's due on Thursday," Mrs. Reynolds was saying. "Yeah, thanks." Pause. "She's here, but she's in a mood." Pause. "I don't know. Go ahead and try."

Me, Vanna realized. She's talking about me and rent money. Who would she . . . Uh-oh.

"Vanna," Mrs. Reynolds called out. "It's your father. Come talk to him."

"Tell him I'm busy," Vanna replied. She turned the volume back up on the television. "Tell him I don't have anything to say to him."

Her mom walked into the living room, turned off the TV, dropped the phone on Vanna's lap, and went back to her room.

"Yeah," Vanna said into the phone.

"Hi, honey, how are you?" Her father's voice was cheerful.

"Great," she answered. So much better without you around.

"Good. Good. Your mom said you're making friends."

"I already had lots of friends."

"I know. How's school?"

"Great," Vanna said with mock enthusiasm. "We have to use see-through backpacks to make sure no one brings a gun to school. We aren't allowed to use lockers because someone might keep a gun in there. And every few days there's a fight in the cafeteria. Loads of fun."

"Maybe we should see about putting you in a private school."

"Oh, yeah, a tiny school with no football team or marching band. Better yet, how about an all-girls school. I could be really miserable there."

"So you like being in marching band?"

"No." What was his problem? Did he think she could pretend everything was okay? "Why did you call?"

"Well, your birthday's coming up. I thought I could drive down and we could do something," Mr. Reynolds said hesitantly.

"I'm spending my birthday with Mom."

"I know, but maybe after that. I haven't seen you since June."

"Don't bother."

"Oh, come on. We could—"

"Really. I don't want you to come," Vanna said firmly.

"Vanna, you don't mean that."

"I do," Vanna insisted.

"I know you're angry, but we'll never get through this if you don't talk to me." He sighed. "At least talk to your grandma. She doesn't live that far from you."

"I don't think that's a good idea," Vanna said. Her dad's mom lived in San Antonio, but the woman didn't talk to Vanna. She criticized. She didn't like the way Vanna dressed or did her makeup, or her attitude.

"Vanna, I don't know what you want me to say."

"I don't want anything from you. Why don't you get back to Janet," Vanna said, then hung up. He was trying to make himself feel less guilty and she wasn't going to let him.

"Talking to him gets easier the more you do it," Mrs. Reynolds said from the doorway of her bedroom.

"Can you believe him? Why doesn't he leave us alone?"

"Vanna, I can't do this right now. Dahlia's on her way to pick me up."

Vanna just flipped on the TV in response.

Fatima stepped into the chilly pool. She was already freezing because the pool area was cold. She began shivering as she waded into the water. This was not how she wanted to spend her Sunday evening, but her mother was excited. The woman really needed to get out more.

"*Ay!*" her mother said when she joined Fatima. "*Tienes frio, mi'ja?* Oh, your lips are turning blue. Quick, swim around so you warm up."

Fatima started jogging. She could feel the fat on her thighs rippling. It was disgusting. She had stuffed herself into one of those tummy-minimizing swimsuits, hoping to minimize her humiliation at being dragged to water aerobics with her mother. In Fatima's opinion, purposely subjecting yourself to a class filled with scantily clad overweight people was just wrong.

Before that evening, Fatima hadn't worn a swimsuit since she was nine years old, and didn't even own one. She hated bathing suits and hated trying them on even more. For some reason, her mother had had mercy on her and bought her an expensive suit from JCPenney. The swimsuit was supposed to make tummy fat disappear, but all it did for Fatima was squeeze her fat so it came out in weird places like her back and under her arms.

"Everybody ready? Let's get started!" a well-toned African-American woman said as she turned on some oldies music. "Now jog. Pump your arms," she instructed, demonstrating the moves.

"You okay?" her mother asked as they started doing underwater jumping jacks.

"Yeah, it's not hard," Fatima responded, but she was beginning to think otherwise.

"You're supposed to suck in your *panza*," Mrs. Garcia said, and poked Fatima's stomach.

"I am," Fatima insisted, her jaw clenched. She was holding in her stomach, but it didn't seem to do much good. She could still feel her belly bouncing around.

"Well, that's why we're here, to get you skinny. It'll get better," her mother said.

Funny, Fatima thought, I don't see a single skinny person here. You'd think that if water aerobics really worked, the people in this class would be in better shape.

The first half hour dragged. Fatima was frustrated. She couldn't seem to do anything right, and her mother's constant comments only irritated her more. But after a while, she got into it. For once in her life, Fatima felt graceful. She'd taken dance classes with Olivia in seventh grade, but had quit after two lessons. She couldn't stand looking at herself in a leotard and tights, and the studio had too many full-length mirrors. But, hopping through the water, she could imagine she was a ballerina gliding across a stage. Then the image of the dancing hippos from *Fantasia* came into her mind and took all the joy out of the moment.

As soon as class ended, she rushed out of the pool. She hated how she felt increasingly heavy. Gravity: God's cruel joke to remind her how fat she was. She walked as fast as she could to her locker, grabbed her clothes, and found a bathroom stall to change in. She hated being fat.

"That was fun, *no*?" her mother said on their way to the car.

"Yeah, whatever," Fatima said. Her mother had a twisted sense of fun, Fatima thought as she got into the brown 1979 Lincoln Town Car.

The car had definitely seen better days. The air-conditioning didn't work and the antenna had long ago disappeared. Fatima's dad had jammed a wire hanger into the antenna base, which allowed the car to pick up three, sometimes four, radio stations.

"I'm only trying to help you," Mrs. Garcia snapped at her.

"Yeah, I know, *Mami*, I'm sorry. It's just . . . I'm frustrated. Why should I even bother? I'm gonna be fat for the rest of my life. It's heredity. Look at you and Papa," Fatima said.

"Fatima!"

"Sorry, but it's true." Maybe it was mean, but Fatima was tired.

"I had five babies! That's what happened to me. When I was your age, I was tiny. I don't understand why you're so fat. I think maybe you don't move enough."

"My diet isn't that great either. Your cooking isn't exactly low-fat, you know."

"But your brothers aren't fat. Neither are your . . . Neither is Lourdes," her mother said.

Fatima knew her mother had almost said "sisters." Fatima had two sisters, nine-year-old Lourdes and seventeen-year-old Guadalupe, but no one ever talked about Lupe. When Lupe ran away, she was cut out of their lives.

"Thanks for pointing that out," Fatima said, staring out the car window.

Mrs. Garcia sighed. "I'm only trying to say that you can't blame my cooking. I was raised on rice and beans and I wasn't fat. Luli and the boys eat the same things as you and they're skinny."

"I have a slow metabolism."

"Ah," her mother said dismissively, "you're lazy. If you do something besides watching TV, maybe you lose weight."

"I do! I march every day in band. That's a workout." Fatima couldn't believe how dense her mother was sometimes.

"I thought it would help, but . . . Maybe if you played a bigger instrument, like your friend with the red hair."

"Can we not do this now? I'm tired, and I still have a ton of stupid homework to do this weekend." Fatima had reached a breaking point, which clearly her mother didn't notice.

"Don't say that word. It isn't nice," her mother said.

Fatima knew her mother hated the word *stupid*. *Stupid* was considered a very rude word in Spanish, but in English it was all right. Everyone said it, even teachers. Fatima had tried explaining that, but her mother never listened. She was convinced Fatima was being corrupted. So Fatima tried to work *stupid* into every conversation to desensitize her mother. Annoying her was a fringe benefit.

They pulled into the driveway. Mrs. Garcia turned to Fatima and suggested, "Maybe you could put plastic wrap around your stomach. That way you could sweat away your *panza* while you do your homework."

"*Mamá! Ya!* Stop it already," Fatima yelled. She burst out of the car, slamming the door shut behind her.

In the house, Fatima found her brothers and sister eating *ojarascas* and watching television. Juan and Diego, hyperactive three-year-old twins, could eat whatever they wanted and not gain an ounce.

She reached for a small sugary cookie and heard her mother say, "Don't. You want to undo all the work we did? Do you like being fat?"

"Yeah, I love it!" she said, and stuffed the whole cookie into her mouth, then stomped to her room.

Of course, it wasn't only her room. All the children shared one room. Juan and Diego slept in one set of bunk beds, and Fatima and Luli in the other. The dresser drawers were so stuffed they were impossible to close. There were three tortilla-sized scorch marks on the shaggy green carpet where Juan and Diego had tried to start "campfires." It didn't look like a bedroom. It looked like a dump.

Fatima put on her Beatles CD and grabbed her Algebra II book. There was no desk in the room so she sprawled out on her bed and opened the book. She was taking eleventh-grade math as a freshman. At this rate, she would be able to take college-level courses in her junior year. You'd think that would be enough, but no, her mother seemed more concerned with Fatima's weight than with her brain.

As if on cue, her mother appeared in the doorway. "Fatima, I thought you might like to try the plastic wrap."

"Fine, I guess it can't hurt." Fatima stood.

"Let me help you put it on."

Fatima lifted her shirt and her mother began winding the plastic around Fatima's waist.

"I don't like making you feel bad. I just want you to be happy and healthy. Now," her mother said, after she tore the plastic wrap and patted it into place, "finish your homework." She kissed Fatima on the forehead and left.

Fatima didn't know why she bothered trying to lose weight. She wasn't trying to attract anyone. She'd never even let herself crush on anyone, knowing that she would only be disappointed.

3

"My birthday's next Wednesday. Do you want to go to dinner with my mom and me? It's on my mom," Vanna asked as the girls poked at their lunches: greasy bits of turkey in gravy.

"I didn't know your birthday was coming up," Olivia said. "Dinner sounds great."

"I'm in if it's okay with my parents. But I have to ask when they're in a good mood since it's a school night," Fatima said.

"Hey, girls," Alex said, sliding into the empty chair next to Vanna.

"Hi, Alex," Fatima said.

"Alex, are you taking anyone to the band's homecoming dance?" Vanna asked.

Alexander Hamilton High School had banned school-wide dances because of fighting, but the band was allowed to have its own dances for fund-raising. Only band members were supposed to go, but pretty much anyone who paid for a ticket could get in.

"Are you asking me?" Alex said.

"Nope," Vanna said with a laugh.

"It's three weeks away. Give me some time," Alex said. "Y'all have dates?"

"We don't need dates," Vanna said. "It's not like prom or anything."

"Fatima says she's not even going," Olivia added.

"You guys know I hate dances," Fatima said.

"But it's our first high school dance," Olivia protested. "This is going to be so much better than anything in middle school."

"It's a band dance," Alex said. "You've got to go. You wouldn't wanna miss the tuba players trying to dance to hip-hop. It'll be hilarious."

"That would be interesting." Fatima agreed. She didn't want to admit it, but she did sort of want to go to the dance.

"Besides," Alex said, "if you don't go, who's gonna help me get the DJ to play some decent music? You know they only listen to girls."

Fatima started to say DJs only listen to pretty girls, but stopped herself. No need to point out the obvious. Luckily, at that moment, Alex spotted Travis two tables away and started teasing Olivia, making her blush and giggle.

All conversation halted when Carlos Jones, a junior, walked up to the table.

"You're in my math class, right?" he asked Fatima. She nodded.

"What's your name again? Sorry, I'm horrible with names."

"It's Fatima," she said. What was this guy doing talking to her? He was gorgeous. With his big dark eyes and slicked-back black hair he looked like he'd stepped out of some fifties movie. Never in a million years did she think he would ever talk to her.

"Well, um, could I talk to you in private for a second?" Carlos asked.

Carlos Jones wanted to talk to her in private?

"Sure," she said, rising. Vanna and Olivia were grinning at her like idiots.

"You know, I'm in this band Pulgas. You've heard of us, right?" Carlos said. He placed his hand on the back of her left arm and guided her to a deserted corner of the cafeteria by a broken vending machine.

"Yeah, I think I might have," she said. Of course she had! Everyone talked about them.

"Well, we have this gig at the White Rabbit next Saturday, and I thought you might like to come and watch us."

"That'd be cool," she replied casually—or what she hoped was casually.

"I was kinda hoping you could help us out a little," Carlos said while looking into her eyes.

Fatima's heart started racing. What was happening to

her? She wasn't the type to swoon over a guy. That was more Olivia's thing.

"Help? How?" she asked.

"You know, with midterms coming up, teachers are really piling on the work. And this gig on Saturday is important. It could be our big break, you know? So, we have to practice a lot."

"Hmmm, I can imagine," Fatima said, trying not to stare at his lips. They were so perfect.

"Yeah, so I was wondering if you could help us out with some homework and stuff."

"Me? What could I do? I'm just a freshman."

"Yeah, but you're real smart. We're in the same math class and everything. And you're always reading."

"Not always," Fatima protested. She read only when she finished her work early. Nobody in that class talked to her, so it wasn't like she had anything else to do.

"I bet you already read *Macbeth*, right?" Carlos smiled at her again.

Fatima started to say no, but stopped herself. He looked so vulnerable. She sighed. "What do you want me to do?"

"Well, I've got this major paper due on Thursday, and I haven't had a chance to read the play. If you could just type something on *Macbeth*, it would really save my life."

"I don't know . . . we could get in big trouble . . ." she said. Doing his homework for him. The idea went against everything Fatima believed in. But out of all the people in school he had asked her, chubby Fatima Garcia.

"I could get you backstage passes. Please. I need you, Fatima," Carlos said. He pushed a lock of hair behind her ear then slid his hand down her face, cupping her cheek for a moment. The warmth of his hand, the texture of his skin, his scent, and the nearness of him filled her senses, oversaturating her brain with hypnotic sensations. Why was she even hesitating?

"All right, I'll do it," Fatima said.

"I knew I could count on you. I'll give you the assignment and some notes tomorrow after school. Where do you hang out?"

"I have flute practice after school on Wednesdays."

"Okay, I'll give it to you then." He shrugged slightly.

"But what if someone sees us?" Fatima worried.

"Don't worry. I'll say I needed to talk to you about math or something. No one will care. So, you'll be in the band hall?"

"Yeah."

"See you then," Carlos said. And then he was gone.

Fatima felt stunned.

"So? What was all that about?" Vanna asked, as Fatima rejoined her friends.

"Oh, nothing much," Fatima mumbled.

"Come on! You just had a lengthy conversation with Carlos Jones. You've got to tell us about it," Olivia said.

"Okay, okay. He wants me to help out with his band," Fatima said, smiling.

"Really?" Olivia asked.

"You?" Alex said.

"How?" Vanna wondered.

"I'm gonna help them with homework, and I'll get a backstage pass to their gig at the White Rabbit," Fatima answered.

"Wow," Olivia marveled.

"What are you gonna do? Tutor them?" Vanna asked.

"Yeah, something like that," Fatima said. She didn't want to tell her friends the truth.

"That doesn't make sense. No offense," Alex said, "but why did he ask you?"

"Because he thinks I'm smart," Fatima snapped.

"And gullible," Alex added.

"What? You can't believe that Carlos Jones would want to talk to me? That he would be interested in me? Because I'm fat, and nobody likes fat girls, right?"

"No, that's not what I meant—" Alex started, but Fatima interrupted.

"Right! Well, I've got news for you, *little* boy. Not all guys are intimidated by a girl who has brains."

"Hey, I'm not like that."

"Really?" Fatima challenged.

"You know what? Forget it. I thought he might be taking advantage of you. But I guess you want him to. Go be his slave, see if I care," Alex said quietly. He slid back his chair, got up, and walked off.

The girls stood. Olivia made sure to push in Alex's chair.

"Don't worry about him. Think about Carlos. I saw him touching your cheek. What was it like?" Olivia asked, hooking her arm through Fatima's as they started out of the cafeteria.

"Yeah, give us the details. What did his hands feel like? Did he give you his phone number? Are you going to call him?" Vanna said, grabbing Fatima's other arm.

Fatima knew she should love that for once she was getting the attention. The skinny girls were begging her for the details. In a few minutes, she had gotten further with Carlos than Olivia had gotten in three years of near conversations with Travis. Stupid Alex. She couldn't even enjoy her big moment because he had to go and mess things up.

4

Vanna sat on the wide steps leading up to the school's main entrance. It was past six and most of the students and teachers had gone home. Vanna liked the quiet, spooky sadness of the nearly deserted school. It made her feel that if she sat there long enough, she could figure out the meaning of her meaningless life.

She checked her watch for the fifth time. Where was her mother? Vanna had been sitting there for almost half an hour.

"Hey, all by yourself?" Alex said, easing down next to her.

"Looks like it," she said. "Why are you still here? I thought just the flutes had after-school practice today?"

"I decided to join the Environmental Club. Your mom forget about you or what?"

"Probably." Vanna sighed. "I only reminded her three times this morning."

"Maybe she's stuck in traffic," Alex offered.

Vanna shrugged.

"Parents can really suck sometimes," Alex said.

"Where's your dad?"

"He's coming from work. He'll be here eventually. Have you called your mom?"

"Yeah," Vanna said. "Her phone's off. She probably forgot to charge it."

"Got anyone else you can call?" he asked.

"No." She had used up all her money on the pay phone. Now she couldn't even take the bus. "I'm sure she'll be here at some point."

Alex pulled a book out of his backpack. "I came prepared to wait," he said.

Alex was sort of cute. His black hair would look decent if he didn't shellac it with gel and spike it in an odd porcupine-ish way. He did have gorgeous hazel eyes and long lashes hidden behind his glasses. Even when she piled on mascara, Vanna's eyelashes never looked that good.

"So, um, does your book have a map in the front?" Vanna asked.

"Yeah, why?"

Vanna giggled. "Fatima told me anytime she needs to buy you a gift, all she has to do is look for a book with a map."

He snorted. "She would notice that."

"I guess she pays attention to what you read."

He shrugged and said, "Or maybe it's just that we've known each other forever."

"In all this time, you've never hooked up with Fatima or Olivia?" Vanna had been wondering about that since she met them. Girls and guys just didn't stay friends that long without something happening. "They not your type or what?"

"Olivia's only had eyes for Travis for years," Alex replied, finally looking up from his book. "And, while I think somebody needs to show her that Travis is not God, I'm not that man."

"And Fatima?"

"Fatima knows everything. She can argue circles around anybody. She doesn't do that passive-aggressive stuff. If you're being *necio*, she lets you know it."

"*Necio?*" Vanna asked. Great, another Spanish word thrown into conversation like she was supposed to know what it meant. Would she ever fully understand San Antonio–speak?

"It means 'annoying.' She tells me I'm *necio* a lot."

"You almost sound like you're complimenting her."

"Maybe. I don't know. She used to be like that until this year. Now she suddenly turned into a girl."

"Um, Alex, you only recently noticed that?" Vanna laughed.

"You know what I mean," Alex said. "What's with her

new stupidness? That stuff with Carlos at lunch. Why is she making a fool of herself over him?"

Vanna hadn't noticed Fatima doing anything foolish. "You don't think he's good enough for her?"

"It's not just that," Alex answered. "I never would have pictured her with someone like him. I didn't think looks and popularity were important to her."

"Who did you picture her with?" With someone like you? Vanna wondered.

"I don't know," Alex mumbled, turning back to his book. "Someone smarter."

"Hey, we don't know he's not smart."

"Yeah, right. What could they have in common? What would they talk about?"

"I don't know. Relax, it's not that big a deal," Vanna said.

"He just doesn't seem her type," Alex said.

Vanna couldn't resist objecting. "I think he's everybody's type."

Carlos was the type of guy Vanna would have dated back home, but in San Antonio she didn't stand a chance with him. Something had happened to her on that drive down I-35 from Plano that had drained the coolness and confidence out of her.

"Maybe, but I think he'll hurt her. I'm sure you could handle him, but I don't see this ending well for her," Alex said.

"Give Fatima some credit. She's tough." Nothing ever

seemed to bother Fatima. Sure, she wasn't happy about her weight, but she didn't whine about it or go on crazy diets. She joked about it.

"I guess." Alex didn't look convinced.

"You think I could date Carlos? I'm flattered."

Alex shrugged. "I said you could handle him. You're good at keeping everyone at arm's length."

"I think you've read one too many self-help books," she said, forcing a laugh. She couldn't figure out if he was complimenting or insulting her.

A blue Ford Taurus pulled up and honked.

"Whatever," Alex said, standing. "That's my dad. You want a ride?"

"Nah, my mom should be here any minute." Vanna hoped that was true. Ever since they had moved here, Mrs. Reynolds had changed. She had become forgetful and self-absorbed.

"Then we'll wait with you," Alex said.

"You don't need to go all chivalrous. I'll be fine by myself," Vanna said.

"Come on," Alex said softly. "It's getting dark. I wouldn't want to stay here by myself."

Her mother might never show up. Vanna didn't need an audience to her loserdom. "I'll take you up on that ride, if your dad doesn't mind," Vanna said.

It would serve her mother right if Vanna wasn't there when she finally bothered to show up. Let her worry. She deserved it.

5

To Olivia, being multicultural meant that her mother could make *picadillo* (seasoned ground beef) one day, Hamburger Helper (ground beef and macaroni) the next day, and spaghetti (ground beef in sauce over noodles) the next. Apparently, every culture in Olivia's background had a meal that could be made cheaply with ground beef. Her mother made these dishes over and over every week with the occasional break for pot roast (when the meat was on sale), and cheese enchiladas (on Fridays during Lent). Her father had never cooked. Maybe if he had, Olivia would have learned some German or Jewish recipes involving ground beef.

Rosa's threat of throwing up if she had to eat any more ground beef, combined with a sale on cow tongue at the grocery store, had prompted their mom to dig up an old family recipe for *lengua*. Olivia had tasted *lengua* once at Fatima's house. It was incredibly tender and delicious once you got over the weird texture. Mrs. Silverstein had never made it for the family before because Olivia's dad wouldn't let her. Since his death, she had occasionally begun experimenting with recipes, tackling such delicacies as *barbacoa* (meat from the head of the cow) and *menudo* (stew made from the stomach of a cow).

However, the family drew the line at certain dishes that Fatima's father had told Olivia were "real" Mexican food. No one in Olivia's family had any desire for *cesos* (brains) or *tripas* (intestines). Fatima's father said Olivia's white blood had diluted her taste buds. Anytime Olivia stayed over at Fatima's house, Mr. Garcia found leftovers of some "real" Mexican dish and tried to make Olivia taste it.

Mrs. Silverstein was supposed to make the *lengua*, but now that she was working two jobs, she didn't have time. So Olivia, figuring she could follow a recipe, decided to make it herself as a surprise. While the *lengua* simmered in the slow cooker, Olivia started on the rice.

"Do you ever watch TV?" Rosa asked, walking into the kitchen. She turned on the television.

"What?" Olivia replied.

"I don't think it's the best idea to space out while chopping stuff," Rosa said. She took a piece of the bell pepper Olivia had been slicing and chomped on it. "I wouldn't want any extra Olivia flavoring in my food."

"Keep your hands off or there'll be some extra Rosa flavoring in tonight's dinner," Olivia said, waving the knife at Rosa.

"Really, Olivia," Rosa said. "You don't even have the radio on. Don't you get bored sighing over Travis all the time?"

"I wasn't sighing," Olivia said. She dumped the bell peppers in the pan with a sizzle.

"But you were thinking about him," Rosa said as she flipped through the channels.

"I was not. Travis isn't the only boy in the world."

"Please. I live with you. I listen to you talk about him constantly. Not to mention the random notes about him you leave lying around."

"I'm sure they're just lying around," Olivia said sarcastically. "Don't you have anything better to do than bother me?"

"Not really. There's nothing on TV, and my dance practice ended early."

"I thought you had a big show coming up."

"We do, but my teacher had to leave early today, so we got a break."

"You could do your homework." Then maybe I won't have to stay up tonight helping you, Olivia thought. Maybe I could actually have some time to sit around and do nothing for once. It seemed like Olivia never had time to relax. She was always multitasking. She hated multitasking. She was no good at it. Her mind would wander, and she'd end up getting nothing done.

"Hello, Olivia," Rosa said. "Did I lose you? I'm starting to worry you may have mental problems."

"I am ignoring you," Olivia responded. She stirred some chopped onions into the mixture. The dogs circled around her legs, panting and generally getting in the way.

"You don't want to accept reality."

"What do you know about reality?" Typical Rosa. She thought she knew everything.

"More than you," Rosa said, "As I was saying while you were off in your own little world—"

"I like my little world." Olivia tossed the dogs a piece of bell pepper. They sniffed, but didn't eat it.

"That's my point."

"There are no sisters there. No cooking, no dishes, no laundry," Olivia said. She added rice to the pan and continued stirring.

"So everyone's naked and eats raw food off the floor? Your mind is more messed up than I thought," Rosa said. "Anyway, this whole Travis thing is stupid. It's starting to get on my nerves."

"Since when?"

"Since forever."

"Forever? You only found out I like him last year because you were eavesdropping," Olivia said, pouring tomato sauce and water into the rice.

"My point is that Travis is a human being like everyone else. And if his sister can be believed, he is a slob who spends way too much time playing video games and can't dance."

"You told his sister?!" Olivia cried. "I don't want him to know I like him."

"Calm down. I didn't tell her anything. She talks a lot. I just listen to her sometimes."

"Still, I would die if he ever found out," Olivia said as she began warming tortillas. She didn't want to talk to her younger sister about her crush. Rosa was way more popular than Olivia, and Rosa was still in middle school.

"You wanna know what I think you should do?" Rosa asked.

"No." But she did kind of wonder.

"Talk to him. Find out how ordinary he is."

Rosa had a point, but there was no way she could talk to Travis. What would she say?

6

What have I gotten myself into, Fatima thought. She was exhausted. She had come home from flute practice on Wednesday and started on homework—Carlos's homework. Fatima had felt great when Carlos "borrowed" her from practice for a "private word." He touched her shoulder, handed her some papers, and smiled at her. The whole flute section practically drooled when he escorted her back to practice and apologized for interrupting. Suddenly, everyone became interested in Fatima. Bianca Castillo (the most popular flute) had even sought Fatima out after practice to find out what was going on with her and Carlos. Fatima loved being able to say vaguely that they were "just friends" and walk off leaving Bianca stammering. She had been waiting all her life for moments like these. Now, staring at her aunt's ancient typewriter, she wasn't so sure.

Typewriters were stupid machines, but her parents

couldn't afford a computer. Her typewriter was so old it didn't even have a delete button. Of course, that didn't really matter since she couldn't think of a single thing to write about the symbolism in *Macbeth*.

Fatima ripped the paper out of the typewriter. She had misspelled *Shakespeare* for the sixth time. At this rate, she would never get to her own homework. What was she going to do?

"Fatima, there's someone at the door for you," her mother said, coming into the kitchen.

"What? Who?" Fatima said. She didn't look up as she loaded a clean sheet of paper into the typewriter.

"It's that little boy from down the street."

"Who?" Her mother called anyone under the age of thirty "little boy" or "little girl." Alex was the only boy on the block who ever came to see Fatima. "If it's Alex, tell him to get lost. I don't have time to deal with him."

"Fatima! *Que lástima!* I'm ashamed of your behavior. He walked all the way over here. Talk to him."

"I don't have time, Mama." The paper crumpled when she hit the return key.

"*No tienes vergüenza?* I see his father every week at church. Go talk to that boy."

"But I have so much to do," Fatima protested, knowing it was useless. Her mother was very big on shame. No one embarrassed Alma Garcia. Just ask Lupe.

"Go! *Andale!*"

"Fine!" Fatima pushed the typewriter away with such force that it almost fell off the kitchen table. Great, Fatima thought, all I need is for it to break.

"*Cuidado*. This thing is older than you are," her mother said.

"I know. That's the problem," Fatima mumbled.

Fatima found Alex in the living room with her brothers, who were immersed in torturing one of their action figures with a hammer.

"Did you want to talk to me or play with Juan and Diego?" Fatima asked impatiently.

Alex said goodbye to her brothers and walked into the hallway with Fatima. "Look, I know I acted like a real butt yesterday. I came over to apologize. I shouldn't have gotten mad at you."

"Yeah, you shouldn't have." He'd given her the cold shoulder since then.

"I don't trust Carlos. I've heard stuff about him. I think he's gonna take advantage of you."

"What do you care?"

"I don't. It's your life, but Carlos is a real jerk."

"Fine. You said your piece. I'm really busy right now," Fatima said.

"We've been friends for a long time," Alex said. "I'm just trying to help."

"I'll be fine. I'm a big girl," Fatima said, and out of habit added, "literally."

"Fatima, don't—" Alex began.

"I know. Thanks, okay?" Fatima said. She couldn't take another lecture on how she was too hard on herself.

"Yeah. Are we cool?" Alex asked.

"Yeah, yeah. Now I really gotta go."

"All right. See you tomorrow," he said.

Fatima got an idea as she watched Alex start toward the front door. "Um, do you know how to use a typewriter?"

"Not really. Why?"

"Never mind. I've got some typing to do, that's all," Fatima said hurriedly.

"What do you need to type?"

"Nothing, just a paper." Fatima instantly regretted saying anything.

"For what class?" Alex asked, looking at her curiously.

"What's with all the questions? Don't worry about it," she snapped.

"What class do you have to write a paper for? I know it's not for English," he said.

"It's none of your business. I'm sorry I asked for your help."

"He's making you do his homework for him, isn't he?" Alex asked. When she didn't answer, he continued, "Don't bother denying it. I should have known. I just didn't think you'd ever do that sort of thing. You're not stupid."

"I'm glad you think so," Fatima said. At least he gave her some credit.

"I don't understand girls. Why would you agree to do something like this? Because he's good-looking?"

"It's not like that! He needed my help," Fatima said meekly.

"Sure." Alex looked doubtful.

"I have a lot of work to do and you're wasting my time. I need to finish."

"Are you really using a typewriter?" Alex asked, his voice softening.

Fatima nodded.

"That'll take forever!"

"I know," she said, tears burning her eyes.

"I've got a computer you could use if you want. It'd be much faster."

"Really? Why do you want to help me?" Hadn't he just said that Carlos was bad and helping him was stupid?

"I don't know. I guess I don't want you to end up flunking and being forced to drop out of band. You are one of the better flutes. Besides, you're gonna make it up to me," he said, smiling.

"I am?" Oh, dear, she thought. More homework?

"Yeah. You're going to lend me your *Beatles Greatest Hits* CD. You know, the one I've been wanting to make a copy of forever."

"That's it?"

"Yeah, but you better hurry up. It's getting late, and I'm not gonna lose sleep over that idiot."

"All right, just give me a sec," she said. She ran to her room for the CD, then went to the kitchen and grabbed her—actually, Carlos's—stuff.

She told her mom that she was going over to Alex's house. Her mother, in the middle of scolding Diego for hitting Juan with a hammer, was too distracted to be suspicious.

Alex and Fatima rushed to his house. He ushered her past the living room, where his dad and younger sister were watching some old western, into Mr. Menchaca's office.

"This is your dad's computer? Are you sure he's okay with me using it?" Fatima asked.

"Yeah, he doesn't care. He won't be using it tonight."

"Okay. Let's get started," she said, sitting down in front of the keyboard. "What do you know about the symbolism in *Macbeth*?"

"Not much," Alex said. He moved his chair next to hers. "You didn't guarantee him an A, did you?"

"No, I didn't," she said and grinned.

They worked surprisingly well together. Fatima had always known Alex wasn't dumb, but she was surprised at how smart he actually was. Must be all those thick books he read. He took over typing when her one-fingered keyboard pecking annoyed him, so they hammered out a semidecent paper in less than an hour.

After thanking Alex several times, Fatima was able to run home, finish her own homework, and get to bed by midnight. She had to share her bed with an already asleep

Diego. Luli had convinced him that *La Llorona* was going to come get him in the middle of the night and drown him in the river. So of course he couldn't sleep by himself. As Fatima tried to fall asleep, she realized she hadn't spent that much time alone with Alex in years. No Olivia to tease or Lupe bossing them around. She'd actually had fun working with him.

7

Vanna set her trombone down and sank back into the couch. The cheerleaders had chosen the theme song from *Indiana Jones* for their high kick routine at Friday's football game. The song was harder than any piece in their halftime show. Vanna wasn't used to having to play lots of eighth notes. She was the bass. Runs were woodwind territory. Vanna was not a naturally talented musician. Just to be the average player that she was required practice. Practice was one of Vanna's least favorite things to do and she put it off as much as possible. But if she didn't memorize this song by Friday, she would have to do a whole lot of push-ups.

The phone rang. Vanna hoped it was Olivia or Fatima so she could put off practicing awhile.

"Hey, girl! What's up?" a voice said in an unmistakable north Texas accent.

"Plano is so boring without you," another voice added before Vanna could say anything.

How Vanna missed her friends' Texas twang. For some reason, San Antonians didn't have typical Texas accents. She hadn't spoken to anyone who had even a hint of twang.

"Where's Caitlyn?" Vanna asked. Usually her three best friends from Plano called Vanna together.

"Um," Ashlee started.

"She had a thing," Taylor said, "but she says hello."

"So, did you find out why Troy hasn't called me?" Vanna asked.

Silence.

"No phone calls, e-mail, nothing," Vanna continued. "I know he's busy, but come on."

"Um," Ashlee said again.

"Tell her, Ashlee," Taylor insisted.

"Why me?" Ashlee squealed. Vanna got the feeling she didn't want to hear whatever Ashlee had to say.

"Because you're better at this stuff."

"I am *so* not, and you know it."

"What are you guys talking about?" Vanna asked.

"We feel so bad about you being exiled and all," Ashlee said. "I still don't get why your mom had to take you to San Antonio."

"She could have at least picked someplace more exciting, like Austin or Houston," Taylor said. "I could totally see you as an Austin girl chasing after hot university guys."

"I already told you she's from here," Vanna said impatiently. "Please, just tell me about Troy."

"How long does your mom need to punish your dad until y'all come back and everything gets back to normal?" Taylor asked.

"It's not like that," Vanna protested. "My parents aren't getting back together. Ever."

"So, what does that mean for you?" Ashlee asked.

"Are you ever coming home?" Taylor pressed.

"I don't think so," Vanna said. "It looks like San Antonio's home now."

"You're not going to like this," Taylor began, "but we think you deserve to know."

"Caitlyn said we could tell you," Ashlee added.

Caitlyn said they could? Had Vanna been like that four months ago? Waiting for Caitlyn's permission?

"Well, then, there's no easy way to say this . . ." Taylor said. "Caitlyn and Troy are dating."

"What?" Vanna practically screamed.

"I know what you're thinking, but nothing went on while you guys were together," Taylor said. "They got close after you broke up."

"Broke up?" Vanna squeaked.

"Yeah," Taylor continued. "When you left. Why didn't you tell us? Instead we had to hear the whole story from Troy."

"You are okay with this, aren't you?" Ashlee asked.

Vanna couldn't believe what she was hearing. She and

Troy hadn't broken up as far as she knew and now she was supposed to be happy that her boyfriend and best friend were dating?

"Of course I'm okay with it. I want them to be happy. I'm moving on also," Vanna replied. She couldn't let them know how upset she was. What was the point?

"Really, do tell," Ashlee said.

Vanna hesitated. There was nothing to tell them. "His name is Carlos. He's a junior, and he's in a band," Vanna lied.

"See, Tay," Ashlee said, "I told you she'd be all right."

"I know. You probably rule the school down there, huh?"

"Um, yeah," Vanna said, dying to change the subject. "So give me the *chisme*."

"The what?" Taylor said.

"You want cheese?" Ashlee asked.

"No, that's what my friends here call gossip."

"*Chisme*, that's cute. Well . . ." Ashlee launched into a long monologue, giving Vanna updates on everybody they knew.

After about twenty minutes of Plano news, Vanna'd had enough.

"You know, it's getting late, and I've got to finish my homework," Vanna said.

"Vanna?" Ashlee giggled. "Since when do *you* do homework?"

"Since now. I've gotta go," Vanna said, and hung up the phone.

What had Troy said to her before she left? She had gone to see him the day before she moved to San Antonio. Caitlyn had come along because she wanted to spend more time with her. Troy had said he would miss her, but he didn't promise to call or come visit. He'd given her a hug. She'd been expecting a kiss. Now that she thought about it, Caitlyn had been standing right there. It made Vanna cringe to remember how Caitlyn had put her arm around Troy's waist and promised to keep an eye on him.

Troy had probably cheated on her. Cheated like her father had. Vanna and Troy had been together only a month or so. She could only imagine what her mother felt like after fourteen years of marriage. Vanna suddenly understood why her mother would move back to San Antonio and try to pick up her life the way it was before she got married. A part of her was glad she'd never have to see Troy or Caitlyn again.

8

The next day an exhausted Fatima yawned her way through band practice. She couldn't seem to stay in step or dredge up the energy to care when she was forced to do push-ups as punishment for her mistakes.

Carlos was so pleased with her work on his paper that he gave her more of his homework, plus his friend Jay's homework. Fatima really had intended to say no. She wasn't going to do his whole band's homework, but Carlos erased her hesitation by promising to take her to dinner in exchange for one more week of help. Her brain (and Alex's computer) had achieved the impossible, a date with the most gorgeous guy she'd ever met.

"There's Taylor and Ashlee," Vanna said, pointing at a picture from her eighth grade graduation dance. Vanna and

Olivia were having a study session at Vanna's, but they hadn't actually gotten to the studying part yet.

"And that's Troy." Vanna pointed to another picture in the album. Vanna had pulled out her albums with the intention of showing Olivia a few pictures, but Olivia had wanted to look at everything. It was kind of fun reliving her past. They went through the braces, bad haircuts, and even Vanna's brief but misguided soccer career.

"Oh, he is handsome," Olivia said. She looked at the photo hoping to find something wrong with Troy. The guy was tan and blond, wearing jeans and a faded shirt that showed off his biceps. "Too bad he's such a jerk, though. Where's Caitlyn?"

"There." It was a picture from Caitlyn's birthday the year before. "Isn't she perfect? Not a hair out of place and no frizz. It's even the perfect color. And that tan makes me sick." Vanna either freckled or burned, but never tanned.

"Actually," Olivia said, "she seems kind of plain to me."

"You think?" Vanna had always thought Caitlyn looked like a model.

"She's dressed so ordinary. Is that the style up there?" Olivia asked.

"Yeah, I guess." Vanna winced at a picture of herself in a bright blue paisley sundress, long dangly silver earrings, and her red hair everywhere. "I go shopping with my mom a lot. Our fashion sense tends to be a little bit loud."

"I like it," Olivia said. "You're way prettier than Caitlyn. Troy is crazy."

Vanna wanted to hug Olivia for being so kind.

"Thanks," she said quietly.

A few minutes later Vanna put the albums away. The girls opened their biology books, intending to start studying seriously, but ended up discussing Fatima.

"Why is Fatima hanging out with Alex tonight?" Vanna wondered.

"I don't get it," Olivia answered. "They've always been good friends, but Fatima hasn't been to his house since sixth grade."

"I thought she liked Carlos. Do you think she'll go with one of them to the band dance?"

"I don't know. You heard Fatima the other day. She doesn't like dances." Hoping to steer the conversation back to biology, Olivia added, "Did you find a definition for *mitosis*?"

"It's on page seventy-three," Vanna said. "We should go together. We could get ready here. It would be fun."

"Sure," Olivia said, copying down the definition.

Vanna took the hint and let the conversation end. They worked in silence for a while. Vanna could take only so much undiluted biology, so she closed her book, stretched, and said, "All this research stuff is making me hungry."

"Yeah," Olivia muttered without looking up from her work.

"We need a break," Vanna said. "Let's see what snack we can find." She headed to the kitchenette.

"We haven't really been working long enough to take a break," Olivia said, but she followed Vanna anyway.

A search of the nearly empty pantry produced some brownie mix. Vanna tore open the mix bag and dumped it into a bowl, releasing the faint odor of chocolate. The scent instantly took Olivia back to the last time she had smelled it.

"The week before my dad died I made him brownies. I don't think I've touched one since," Olivia blurted out, immediately feeling exposed. She didn't think Vanna needed to hear her sob story. "I'm sorry. I didn't mean to make you uncomfortable."

"That's okay. I've never heard you talk about your dad before," Vanna said.

"I don't know why I said anything. I don't like talking about him. It just makes me miss him. It's almost easier to pretend he never existed. I never had a dad so he never died. Does that sound horrible?"

"No," Vanna said. "Sometimes I do the same thing. If you never had a dad he can't leave you."

"My mom doesn't understand that. She always wants to talk about him and I can't."

"My mom wants me to talk about my dad and their divorce. Talking doesn't change the fact that my dad's gone."

"But he can come back," Olivia said. She stirred the brownie batter, trying to tap down the bitterness that bubbled inside her whenever she listened to children of divorce complain. Vanna still had a father—she just didn't like him. "My dad's dead. He can't ever come back."

Olivia took a deep breath and told Vanna the story. "I went to wake him up, and I couldn't. I shook him and even hit him, but nothing worked. I couldn't do it. I screamed for my mom and she called the police. They said we weren't allowed to touch the body. We had to leave him in his boxer shorts. I was so embarrassed for him. The police and paramedics saw him wearing just his underwear. After that, the cleaning started. We had to clean the house because people were coming over with food. Getting more plates dirty, which meant more cleaning." Olivia stopped talking and realized she was crying. She pushed the bowl away.

Vanna quickly took the batter and got Olivia a glass of water. "Here, sit down. I'll put the brownies in the oven," she said.

· "I can still remember the way his skin felt when I tried to wake him. It was different. Different from the way it felt when I kissed him when he was in the coffin." Olivia sipped her water, then said, "As much as my mom wants to talk, when we do, she always ends up crying. And Rosa . . . well, she says she hated my dad."

"I'm sorry," was the only thing Vanna could think to say. She patted Olivia on the back. She wasn't very good at this comforting thing.

"Thanks. I'm okay now. Sometimes stuff just sneaks up on me, you know?"

After Olivia left, Vanna decided to call her dad. It was the right thing to do. What if he was in a car wreck tomorrow and died? Then she'd be in Olivia's boat, only worse.

Vanna dialed her old phone number. As the phone rang she felt her courage dwindle. What was she going to say to him? She found herself hoping that he wasn't home. Then a woman answered. Vanna panicked and hung up.

9

Olivia had never been much of a football fan before, but she was starting to like it. Football would never replace basketball as her favorite sport, but it was hard not to get caught up in the school spirit at the games. The best thing about football games didn't have anything to do with what was happening on the field. It was all about where you sat. Saxophones sat in front of the drumline. Olivia did her best to end up in front of Jake, a snare drummer. It wasn't hard to do. She just had to make sure she was last in line. Jake was good-looking, with his longish black hair falling into his face. And he was cool, always wearing T-shirts featuring indie bands no one had ever heard of, but he was quiet. While the rest of the drumline was forever getting kicked out of practice for acting like fools, Jake was mellow.

Most of the saxes wanted to hang out with the more outgoing drummers. But Jake happened to be Travis Martinez's best friend. There was always a chance that Travis might stop by and talk to him. And there was always a chance that Olivia would turn around and say something incredibly witty and start up a conversation with Travis. So far none of that had happened, but there was always a chance.

Vanna had watched enough Dallas Cowboys games to understand that football was pretty boring. Going to a football game wasn't so much about actually watching it, unless you were in the band. Normal students got to roam around the stadium flirting, gossiping, and stuffing themselves with food from the concession stand. Band members had to sit by section and weren't allowed to eat anything. That wouldn't be so bad if Vanna had friends in her section. But low brass was mostly guys and they mainly talked about the game and/or bodily functions. Neither subject held Vanna's interest.

She had totally messed up on the dance number during the halftime show. A couple of measures into it, her mind went blank and she tried to fake it. Pretending to play the trombone is difficult. Woodwinds wiggle their fingers around so quickly no one can tell if they're faking. But it's pretty obvious when a trombone slide is in the wrong position. At least it felt obvious to Vanna. Why had she even bothered practicing?

Vanna was stuck at the top of the stands with the other loud instruments. Fatima was at the bottom with her section. Olivia and Alex were in the middle of the band.

Vanna's favorite part of the game came just after half-time when the band was allowed to relax and drink some water. During this break the sections mixed. Vanna was able to hang out with her friends until the football team did something goofy like score a touchdown, which meant Vanna would have to race back to her section to play the fight song. Fortunately, that night, touchdowns didn't seem like much of a possibility.

The announcer broke in with an update of a Spurs/Suns preseason game as Vanna scrambled down to the sax section. By unspoken agreement they all met there because, of course, Olivia would never leave her section without permission.

"Sounds like we're missing a great game," Alex said.

"I'm surprised my dad hasn't left yet. It must be killing him to miss it," Fatima said. She had plopped down next to Alex.

"He must really love you," Vanna said.

"I know," Fatima said.

"Don't worry, he's got my dad to commiserate with," Alex said. "He's been checking the score all night."

Vanna looked over to where the band boosters were sitting. Alex's dad was chatting with Fatima's dad and pointing to something on his cell phone. Alex's dad didn't look much like Alex. Mr. Menchaca was handsome. Really handsome. With his wavy black hair, golden skin, and wire-rimmed glasses, he kind of looked like Antonio Banderas crossed with Clark Kent.

"You'd think we could make at least one touchdown," Fatima complained. "I'm really getting sick of hearing 'Dixie.'" "Dixie" was the fight song of Robert E. Lee High School, their competition that night.

"Lee went to the state finals last year. What did you expect?" Alex said. He put his arm around her shoulders. "Cheer up. The more they score, the more their band has to play, and the less we have to do."

"Look who's here," Vanna said.

Carlos Jones was walking down the aisle. He smiled at Fatima and said, "Hey."

Fatima smiled back. Alex dropped his arm from her shoulders.

"How are things going with him?" Vanna asked after Carlos walked off.

Fatima shrugged. "I'm not sure." Carlos didn't seem embarrassed to associate with a freshman band geek. He talked to her in the hallways, the cafeteria, pretty much anywhere. Of course, all their conversations revolved around the work she was doing for him.

"You're awfully quiet," Alex said to Olivia. "Did the game get interesting?"

"Not really," Olivia answered. "Lee's about to score again."

"They might not," a voice said from behind her. His voice. Travis Martinez's voice. When had he sat down behind them? All Olivia had to do was turn around, smile, and either agree or disagree. But Olivia didn't do anything.

After what seemed like forever, Alex came to Olivia's rescue by saying, "Lee's practically in the end zone."

"Where's your school spirit?" Travis asked.

Suddenly, a Hamilton player intercepted a pass and ran clear across the field. No one stopped him. By the time he reached the twenty-yard line everyone was screaming. The guy made the only Hamilton touchdown of the game. Amid all the cheering, before Travis went back to his section, Olivia forced herself to turn around. Travis caught her eye and said, "Told you so."

10

Saturday afternoon, Fatima found herself sitting on a bench in the waiting area of South Garden, a restaurant she'd never been to before. She was meeting her sister for lunch. She was excited, as she missed Lupe. They hadn't talked much in the past seven months since Lupe moved out. Fatima had never even met her niece.

Fatima stood up when she saw her sister. Lupe, who'd never had a weight problem, was now chubby. She had straightened her curly black hair, but still wore her usual heavy eyeliner, dark lipstick, and tight jeans. Fatima couldn't help staring at the baby Lupe was carrying on her hip. The baby had light skin, lots of black hair, and big brown eyes.

"Fati, you don't know how much I've missed you. I see you're still doing the ugly T-shirt and jeans look," Lupe said. She enveloped Fatima in a one-armed hug and kissed her on the cheek.

"Um, you're wearing the same thing, Loops," Fatima said.

Lupe clicked her tongue. "Oh, no. This is just for work. Meet your niece, Chula. Go ahead, take her." She handed Chula to Fatima.

Fatima had held plenty of babies. There were times she felt like she had raised Juan and Diego, but Chula was different. Chula was Lupe's daughter. The baby gurgled at Fatima. "Hello, *chulisima*," Fatima cooed. "What's her real name?"

"Her name is Chula," Lupe said.

"What?" Fatima snapped.

A hostess rushed forward, and greeted Lupe.

"You actually named her Chula?" Fatima hissed as the hostess led them to a table. Chula in English would be something like "cutie-pie."

"Mm-hmm. It fits her. Just look at her," Lupe said. She took Chula from Fatima and put her in a high chair. "All that hair and pretty white skin. She takes after you, *güera*."

It was a joke in the family that Fatima was the lightest. They said it was because Fatima never went out in the sun, which was not true at all. Fatima helped her dad with outside jobs as much as anyone else in the family. If given a choice, Fatima would much rather be in air-conditioning. She wasn't one for lying out in the sun or playing any sort of outdoor sport. One drawback of being in band was that during marching season Fatima got dark.

Lupe smiled and added, "Mama's going to hate the name."

Mrs. Garcia had named her daughters after sites where the Blessed Mother had appeared: Guadalupe, Fatima, and Lourdes. She named her sons for Juan Diego the saint, to whom the Blessed Mother appeared at Guadalupe.

"Mom will most definitely not be pleased," Fatima said. "Tell me about what it's like being a mom."

"I'm lucky. Chula is a perfect baby. Look at that smile. A little flirt like her mama, eh?" Lupe tickled Chula's chin.

When the waiter arrived Lupe ordered for both of them. She said the garlic chicken was delicious. The waiter left after fussing over Chula a little.

"Do you come here a lot?" Fatima asked.

"All the time. I never cook. You should tell Mom to come here. Most of the waiters speak Spanish, and there's a dollar menu for kids under twelve."

"Sure," Fatima said, but she knew her mother would never come. Mrs. Garcia wasn't big on trying different things. Chinese food was a little too exotic.

Enough small talk. Fatima asked, "Are you taking her to the doctor enough?"

"Girl, I go to the doctor more now than we ever did at home," Lupe replied. That wasn't saying much. They almost never went to doctors. All the Garcia kids got their shots at school.

"Ninfa has helped me," Lupe continued.

"Ninfa? Mama's *comadre?*" Fatima asked. Ninfa Morales was Mrs. Garcia's best friend. Ninfa had never married or had kids, but she pretty much adopted the Garcia family.

"Of course. Where do you think I went when I left?" Lupe said.

"I thought you were at your boyfriend's."

"*Phfft.* Yeah, right. I tried that. Eric's parents loved Chula, but not me. So I went to Ninfa's. She takes care of Chula when I go to work."

"And when you're at school, right?" Fatima asked. Lupe was supposed to be a senior at Hamilton. Fatima had assumed Lupe was going to Eric's high school, but she had also assumed Lupe was living with Eric.

"I'm not in school right now. I've got to pay for my car and I'm saving for an apartment. I need to work as many hours as I can. I'll get my GED later on."

"Doesn't Eric help you?"

"He does what he can. He's still in school and working." Lupe shrugged, and Fatima noticed that she looked tired.

"You should come home and let us take care of you."

"And where would we sleep?" Lupe asked. "Don't tell me my bed's just waiting for me?"

"Luli took it, but Diego never sleeps in his bed anymore. Chula should know her family. Why don't you at least visit?"

"Did Mom say she missed me?"

69

Fatima thought about lying, but Lupe would know. Mrs. Garcia wasn't someone who cried about missing anything. "Not exactly, but I know she does. We all do."

"I'm not coming home ever." Lupe could be just as stubborn as her parents.

"Why? I don't understand. Your life would be so much easier."

"No. It would be torture. You don't know. Mama cried when she found out I was pregnant. She said horrible things about me and Dad wouldn't even look at me. Mama said I broke his heart. I won't have them judging me and my baby." Lupe's voice was filled with anger.

"You know if they took one look at her they'd fall in love," Fatima said.

Lupe shook her head. "They saw her in the hospital. And all Mama could talk about was how much the baby was going to cost." Lupe took a deep breath and continued in a much calmer voice, "If Mama misses me so much, she can call me. She can apologize to me. I don't want to talk about them anymore. Tell me about you. How's your boyfriend?"

"My boyfriend?"

"Jando," Lupe said with a knowing smile.

"Oh, Alex." Fatima rolled her eyes. "He's fine and you know he's not my boyfriend." Alex's full name was Alejandro, and until he started school everyone had called him Jando. Their second grade teacher hadn't been able to pronounce Alejandro, so she shortened it to Alex, and from then on everyone at school started calling him Alex. Fatima had always thought her name was bad, but, while people might pronounce it differently, at least they all called her the same thing.

Their food arrived and Fatima filled Lupe in on everything that was happening with Carlos and how Alex was helping her. When they talked about Lupe's friends, Fatima realized that Lupe wouldn't be going to her graduation or doing any of the things seniors obsessed about. Fatima asked if Eric and Lupe were getting married.

Lupe shrugged and looked away. "If he'd propose, maybe."

Fatima caught a glimpse of Lupe's vulnerability before her sister squared her shoulders and started talking about how she didn't need a man to take care of her.

Lupe drove Fatima home, but no matter what Fatima said, she would not go inside the house. Fatima stopped pressuring when she saw tears in Lupe's eyes. She showered Chula with kisses.

"Call me," Lupe said. "I want to know how things turn out with Carlos."

"I will."

They hugged and kissed. Fatima got out of the car. As soon as she shut the door, Lupe sped off. Fatima thought the whole situation was stupid. Lupe said she was happy, but she was struggling. And Fatima knew her parents were worried about Lupe.

Her family was in the kitchen eating lunch. Luli was sitting at the table doing Fatima's usual job, helping Juan and Diego eat. Mrs. Garcia stood at the stove warming tortillas. Mr. Garcia sat at the head of the table, and his sweaty cowboy hat sat next to his plate. They both knew where Fatima had been. Fatima didn't know how, but they knew. Mr. Garcia's eyes, the same dark brown eyes that Lupe had, were filled with a question. A question he was too stubborn to ask.

"She's fine. She's happy," Fatima said quietly.

11

On Sunday evening, Vanna sat between her mother and Dahlia inside a movie theater, staring at the on-screen ads. Mrs. Reynolds had misread the movie times, so they were about half an hour early. Vanna wasn't exactly thrilled to be there. They were seeing some French movie. Vanna's choices were either sit at home and be bored or sit in a theater and be bored. At least there was food at the movies. The Bijou was a theater/bistro, so you could eat a meal while you watched a movie.

Vanna had already gobbled up a Greek veggie pizza, her mother was poking at a salad, and Dahlia was downing latte after latte. Dahlia was a tiny woman with dark hair, eyes, and skin. Beautiful, but full of way too much energy. She was talking a mile a minute.

"So, how are things with Bob?" Dahlia asked Vanna's mom.

Bob. Vanna hated that name. She'd never even met the guy, but already she couldn't stand him.

"Great, we can't get enough of each other." Mrs. Reynolds laughed.

Dahlia joined her. Vanna didn't. Bob was a computer programmer her mother was seeing. As if going out with Dahlia wasn't enough, now her mom had yet another reason not to be home.

"Aren't you happy for your mama?" Dahlia asked.

"I guess," Vanna said, trying not to sound bratty. "But don't you think it's too soon for her to get involved with another guy?"

"Don't worry, honey," Mrs. Reynolds said. "It's nothing serious. I'm just lonely."

Lonely, huh? Maybe if you spent some time with your daughter, you wouldn't be, Vanna thought, but didn't say. She shrugged and excused herself, claiming she needed a soda refill. She left them talking about the crazy stuff they did in college.

In the hall, Vanna spotted Travis and Jake. Jake, who somehow managed to make his theater uniform look cool, was leaning against the wall. Travis was throwing paper in a trash can like he was shooting hoops, but he wasn't very good at it and kept missing.

"I didn't know you guys worked here. How's it going?" she asked as she approached them. So what if she never really talked to either of them at school. Things are different when you see a person outside of school. It would be rude not to acknowledge them.

Travis shrugged. "We're missing the game."

Vanna automatically knew exactly what game: Spurs versus Lakers. Everyone at school had been talking about it. Vanna used to tune out all sports talk, but since moving to San Antonio she'd found it impossible. Everyone talked about the Spurs. Everyone. And basketball season hadn't even really started yet.

"Why aren't you watching the game?" Travis continued. "You're not a Mavs fan, are you?"

"No," Vanna said quickly. She would never own up to that. Vanna knew that one of the most hated people in San Antonio was the owner of the Dallas Mavericks. A few years ago, he had insulted the San Antonio River, and the city still hadn't forgiven him. He was even more hated than Ozzy Osbourne. Back in the 1980s Ozzy had peed on the Alamo.

"Do you know if this movie is any good?" Vanna pointed to the poster for the French movie she was going to see.

"I hear it's weird," Travis said. "I wouldn't have thought you were the boring French movie type."

"Really?" Vanna bristled ever so slightly.

"No offense," Travis said quickly. "Usually I'm the guy that tears the tickets and tells you what theater to go to. I like to see what kind of people go to see certain movies. It's interesting. I would have thought you were a straight-up romantic-comedy girl or maybe some horror."

"Only vampire horror," Vanna corrected. "This movie wasn't my pick."

"You know who I can't figure out?" Travis said.

"Who?"

"Your friend Olivia."

"Olivia?" Perfect, Vanna thought. He thinks about Olivia.

"Yeah," Travis went on. "She comes to see a lot of movies, but all sorts of different ones. Action, romance, horror, freaky independent ones, foreign ones, even kid movies."

Unfortunately, just then, people began streaming out of the theater next to them.

"Duty calls. We better go," Travis said. "C'mon, Jake, let's go earn our money."

"See ya," Jake said to Vanna.

Vanna was in a much better mood when she got back to her mom and Dahlia. They were gossiping about celebrities. Vanna, having spent many hours watching entertainment news programs, was an expert on the subject. She giggled along with them until the movie started. The very long, very strange movie.

As soon as she got home, Vanna called Olivia and recounted word for word her conversation with Travis. Olivia was thrilled, and when Vanna hung up the phone an hour later, she felt better than she had in months.

12

Monday was Mrs. Silverstein's night off. She had promised to cook, but had stayed after school for a faculty meeting, so she hadn't yet started dinner when Rosa ran into the kitchen panicking because she was running late and her ride was waiting outside. Rosa couldn't find one of her dance shoes, and without that specific shoe she would be unable to function. Olivia found the shoe under Rosa's bed while her mom managed to force a peanut butter and jelly sandwich on Rosa.

Olivia and her mother sat quietly for a few moments in the wake of Rosa's frenzied exit.

"Why don't we take the dogs for a walk?" Mrs. Silverstein suggested.

"I'll do it," Olivia said.

"No, it will give us a chance to talk," Olivia's mom replied. "It'll be nice."

Olivia and her mother leashed up the dogs and set out on a leisurely walk around the neighborhood. Mrs. Silverstein talked about all the weird things her fourth graders did. Olivia brought her mom up to date on everything going on with her friends, band, and the evil bio exam she had taken.

"Rosa tells me that you spend most of your time moping."

"What? Rosa exaggerates. You know that," Olivia reminded her mom. "Rosa needs to mind her own business."

"She's worried about you, and so am I. You've gotten so quiet since your dad died. At first I thought it was your way of dealing with it, but you haven't seemed to bounce back."

"I like to daydream. That's all," Olivia scoffed.

"I think you should start taking dance classes again."

"Mom, I barely have enough time for schoolwork as it is," Olivia said.

"Just one class a week. It'll be good for you. And it'll give you and Rosa something in common."

"Great," Olivia said. Because bonding with her know-it-all little sister was such a priority for her.

"Performing might help you get over your shyness," Mrs. Silverstein offered.

Shyness was Olivia's biggest obstacle with Travis. She would do anything to be more confident. If she hated it, she could always say her grades were suffering, and her mom would let her quit. "Okay," she agreed, "one class."

13

That week, Carlos gave Fatima plenty of work to do. On Tuesday, Fatima rushed home from school and convinced her mother to let her have dinner at Alex's.

She hadn't eaten there in years. The Menchacas had something she never ever had at her house: junk food. It was at Alex's house that Fatima was first introduced to such delicacies as chicken nuggets, pudding, macaroni and cheese, and Twinkies. Fatima's mom thought junk food was a waste of money. According to Mrs. Garcia, if the family wanted cookies she could make them. Fatima wanted Chips Ahoy! and Oreos, not *empanadas* and *pan de huevo*.

To Fatima's disappointment, Mr. Menchaca was preparing a home-cooked meal.

"Why don't y'all set the table?" Mr. Menchaca asked. "Dinner'll be ready in a minute."

"We're waiting on the bread sticks," Natalia announced. Alex's little sister, Nati, was about nine years old, and was stick-thin like Alex. She had the same hazel eyes and black hair, but didn't wear glasses.

Alex groaned. "Are you ever going to get tired of them?"

Nati shook her head.

"We eat bread sticks every night," he explained to Fatima. He rumpled Nati's hair and told her, "We spoil you too much."

"I know." Nati smiled.

Fatima helped Alex set the table while Mr. Menchaca and Nati threw together a salad.

"So, Fatima, you've been coming over a lot lately. Is this going to be a regular occurrence?" Alex's dad asked too casually.

"We're working on a project," Alex said quickly.

"Well, it's nice to have you around again," Mr. Menchaca said.

"Is she your girlfriend now?" Nati asked Alex.

Alex blushed. "Like I said, we're just doing homework. Shouldn't you go check on your bread sticks?"

Nati giggled.

Dinner was more of the same.

"Alex doesn't bring friends over very often," Mr. Menchaca said after Nati made another girlfriend comment.

"I wonder why?" Alex mumbled.

After dinner, Alex and Fatima got to work. Fatima couldn't help noticing how close she was to Alex. So close that their arms would brush against each other or sometimes their legs would bump. Alex didn't seem to notice, but Fatima did. What was wrong with her?

She got up and walked around the office. She stopped to look at a photo of Alex's mom holding a baby. A little boy was wrapped around one of her legs.

"Your mom was gorgeous," Fatima said, picking up the picture. She could see the resemblance in Nati, who would no doubt grow up to look just like her pretty mother.

"Yeah," he said. He got up and stood next to Fatima. "I don't remember her ever looking like this. In all of my memories, she's sick. She was always so sick."

Alex turned back to the computer. "I think Carlos's history report is ready to print."

"That was fast," Fatima said. "We're getting good at working together."

"It's been pretty cool just the two of us."

"Yeah," Fatima agreed, feeling awkward. The silence hung heavy in the room. Usually there was never silence between them.

"I'll be right back," Alex said, leaving the room.

Fatima felt off balance. She liked Carlos Jones, and was going on a date with him—someday—but there was something going on with her and Alex.

"For old times' sake," Alex said when he returned. He

had two cream-filled chocolate cupcakes and two cold cans of Big Red soda.

"Yum," Fatima said. She bit into the cupcake and almost reached for the equally calorie-laden soda. "I'll just go get some water," she forced herself to say.

"Thought you were a Big Red girl," Alex said.

"Not anymore," Fatima said, pointing to her stomach and grinning.

"Fatima, I get the whole 'I'm gonna laugh at myself before you can' thing. I do it, too, but you need to stop. You make things—"

"When do you laugh at yourself?"

"All the time. Hello, I'm the geekiest nerd that ever was. Anyway, you're too smart to be beating up on yourself. It seems like ever since you started hanging out with Vanna you've changed."

"Huh?" Fatima said eloquently.

"She has you drinking diet soda, and wearing more makeup. You don't need a makeover."

What was Alex talking about? "Vanna doesn't have me doing anything. I'm just making a few changes."

"I think you're pretty amazing just the way you are."

Fatima didn't know what to say. She could tease Alex for being so corny, but something about the look on his face told her he was being sincere.

She shrugged and started packing up her stuff.

Alex handed her Carlos's paper.

"Thanks again," Fatima said.

"No problem. Just leave me your English notes. I've been kinda zoning in that class, and you always seem to be writing stuff down. They've got to be pretty good."

Fatima handed the notes to him, and left feeling like she didn't understand anything anymore.

14

"Happy birthday," a girl from Vanna's English class said as she stapled a dollar to the dollars already attached to Vanna's shirt.

"Thanks," Vanna replied. It had been happening all day. As soon as Cecelia found out it was Vanna's fifteenth birthday she borrowed Mr. Gutierrez's stapler and stapled a dollar to Vanna's shirt. Cecelia played trumpet in band, but she and Vanna weren't really friends, so Vanna was surprised by the gesture. Then someone else saw the dollar and gave Vanna another. By lunchtime, she had a decent-sized money corsage. It was enough to make a girl feel kind of special.

"What's with the money thing?" Vanna asked Olivia. "Is this like some sort of Hispanic tradition I don't know about?" There seemed to be a lot of those.

"I don't think so. Everybody does it."

"No one in Plano ever stapled dollars to me," Vanna pointed out.

"I guess it's a San Antonio thing," Olivia said.

"I could get used to this," Vanna said. She had to have at least ten dollars.

"Next year not as many people will give you money," Olivia said. "You're turning fifteen. That's a big deal. Most girls have *quinceañeras*."

"Which are?"

"When a girl turns fifteen, she can have a special mass said for her. It's kind of like a wedding. You pick fifteen girls to stand in the ceremony like bridesmaids. You get to wear a poofy white dress and have a huge party afterward. The whole thing means you're a woman."

"Are you going to have one?" Vanna asked. It sounded cool.

"No," Olivia said, "*quinceañeras* are a Hispanic thing. People would laugh if a Silverstein had one." A fact that Rosa didn't seem to care about. She was already planning hers.

"Fatima will, right?"

"I don't think so. Lupe had one, but her escort was Eric, who later became the father of her baby. You can imagine her parents aren't too anxious to have another *quinceañera*. Besides, it's kind of expensive," Olivia said.

"Ow!" Olivia cried. Vanna had elbowed her hard in the ribs. "What was that for . . ." She trailed off when she turned to see what Vanna was looking at. Travis Martinez was walking down the hall behind them. As usual, Olivia's heart started beating faster and her skin tingled. She knew she was turning red. Her cheeks felt warm. Her whole body felt warm.

"Oh, God, he's whistling," Vanna whispered. "How dorky."

"Shh," Olivia managed to say.

Then Vanna did the most horrifying thing Olivia could imagine. She called, "Hey, Martinez. When did you become a loner?"

"Ms. Fielding kept me after class to talk about not living up to my potential, and my friends ditched me," he answered.

He kept coming toward them.

Olivia shot Vanna a panicked look.

"Relax," Vanna whispered. "Here's your chance. Remember to talk Spurs and movies."

"Where's the third amigo?" Travis asked when he caught up to them.

Vanna waited for Olivia to say something in response, but when she didn't, Vanna answered, "Good question. She's probably with Alex somewhere."

Olivia listened to Travis chat with Vanna. He wished her a happy birthday and asked about her plans. Vanna, being a good friend, subtly tried to shift the conversation over to Olivia. Vanna was smiling and laughing, totally at ease and charming. Why couldn't she be more like Vanna?

"I think our sisters are fighting," Travis said to Olivia.

"Your sisters know each other?" Vanna asked.

Olivia took a deep breath and tried not to think about how perfect Travis looked, and said, "They go to the same school. They're both in pep squad."

"And admit it," Travis said, looking at Olivia, "they hate each other."

He is a normal human being, Olivia told herself before his smile could make her forget how to talk again. "Right now they do, but it won't last. They were best friends a few weeks ago."

"I hope so because Virginia's complaining is driving me crazy. She wanted me to talk to you about it."

Olivia decided she loved Travis's sister.

Travis continued, "Something about Rosa not taking pep squad seriously. Apparently, Rosa said it was dancing for robots and that any moron could do it. Virginia got real upset. I don't know what you're supposed to do about that."

Olivia decided she loved Rosa.

"I'll talk to her," Olivia promised. "Sometimes Rosa says stuff without thinking."

"Thanks." Travis smiled at her.

"Are you going to the homecoming dance or do you have to work?" Vanna asked him out of the blue. It was a blunt transition, but there was no time for subtlety. Vanna did not have Olivia's patience. She was ready to move things along, and the dance would be the perfect opportunity to bring Olivia and Travis together.

"Yeah. Are y'all?"

"Um," Olivia faltered. The power of speech had once again deserted her.

"C'mon, I know dances are lame, but it's better than staying home," Travis said.

"Of course we are." Vanna answered.

"Good, I'll see y'all there. And, Olivia, thanks again for the help with Virginia. I've gotta go look for my reject friends." Then he was gone.

Olivia was definitely going to that dance.

Vanna's birthday dinner was at Chart House, the restaurant at the top of the Tower of the Americas. The tower reminded Vanna of something out of the Jetsons. It was basically a long column supporting a round object that resembled the bottom half of a barrel with an antenna on top.

The girls drank in the view from the glass elevator as they rose higher and higher.

When Vanna stepped into the restaurant, she felt as if she had stepped into another city. A more sophisticated city, like New York or Los Angeles. There were huge windows everywhere, and the restaurant rotated slowly to display an ever-changing view.

The hostess seated them and a waiter appeared to take their drink orders. When the waiter returned with their drinks, Vanna's mom proposed a toast.

"To my beautiful Vanna. Happy fifteenth," Vanna's

mother said, lifting her glass of iced tea. Olivia and Fatima clinked their glasses with Vanna's.

"Open your presents before we do anything else," Vanna's mother ordered excitedly.

"Olivia's first," Fatima said.

Vanna ripped open the package, revealing a DVD of *Sixteen Candles*.

"I know you're not sixteen yet," Olivia explained, "but it is the greatest movie ever made."

Fatima's present was a photo album. On the first page was a picture of the three of them in their uniforms at a football game.

"For all your new memories," Fatima told Vanna.

"Cool, *Buffy*," Fatima said when Vanna opened the gifts from her mother. She had given Vanna the boxed sets of a few seasons of *Buffy the Vampire Slayer*.

"Thanks, Mom. Season two's my favorite. It's so romantic." Vanna hugged her mother.

"I know," Mrs. Reynolds said. Vanna smiled. Her mom had picked out the perfect gifts. Maybe she wasn't as oblivious as Vanna had thought.

"So, we need a plan for Olivia and Travis at the dance," Vanna announced after the waiter had taken their dinner orders.

"Who is Travis?" Vanna's mother wanted to know.

"He's the boy Olivia's madly in love with," Vanna answered. She was in such a good mood—the restaurant was perfect, the presents were awesome, and she loved celebrating with Olivia and Fatima. She was even having a great time with her mom.

"But he doesn't even know I exist," Olivia added.

"He *so* does. Y'all were just talking today," Vanna said.

"Olivia's really shy around him," Fatima explained to Mrs. Reynolds.

"You want my advice?" Mrs. Reynolds asked.

"No, Mom, please," Vanna said. Her mother's advice was not so motherly. Vanna did not want her mother sharing her cuter-is-always-better theory: all men are self-centered cheaters, so you might as well find one that's nice to look at while it lasts.

"Be yourself," Vanna's mother told Olivia.

Vanna was surprised. That was pretty normal advice.

"And if that doesn't work, then forget about him," Mrs. Reynolds continued.

"What?" Olivia said.

"There are too many men out there to waste time on one who doesn't appreciate you. How long have you wasted on this guy?"

Olivia looked down, feeling embarrassed.

"Three years," Fatima said. "Although to be fair, Olivia hasn't really been being herself around him. But let's talk about the birthday girl. Who are you hoping to dance with at homecoming, Vanna?"

Olivia sighed in relief. Trust Fatima to come to her rescue.

"I don't know," Vanna said. The only guys she talked to at school were Alex and Travis.

"There has to be someone you like," Olivia said.

"You can't tell me there's no one interesting at your school," Mrs. Reynolds said.

"I really haven't been looking for anyone," Vanna said. She was still kind of hung up on Troy.

"Isn't there any guy you'd be willing to dance with?" Olivia pressed.

Vanna quickly picked out a guy. "Jake's cool."

"Okay." Olivia smiled. "You talk to Jake, and I'll talk to Travis. Deal?"

"Sure," Vanna agreed.

"I almost forgot. Here." Fatima handed them bracelets made of plastic beads that spelled out "Go Spurs Go." "Alex's sister made them for us."

"That's sweet. I've never even met his sister," Vanna said.

"The poor thing thinks I'm cool," Fatima said.

"You've been spending a lot of time at Alex's house lately," Olivia said.

"Is there something you want to tell us?" Vanna asked.

"It's not what you're thinking," Fatima protested. "He's just helping me with some work."

"Uh-huh," Vanna said.

"No, really. That's all. But guess what? Carlos asked me out."

"Wow," Olivia said. "Where are you going?"

"I'm not sure."

"When's y'all's date?" Olivia asked.

"He hasn't exactly said, but soon." That sounded lame even to Fatima. Vanna and Olivia looked skeptical. Mrs. Reynolds seemed to be very interested in stirring her tea. The Carlos date would probably never become a reality, but at least he offered. That was more than any other guy had done.

"Does Alex know about it?" Vanna asked.

"No. Why would he care?" Fatima said, but a part of her knew he would.

15

On Thursday night, Alex asked Fatima out on a date.
Sort of.

They were taking a break from another one of Carlos's
papers and were talking about Lupe.

"Lupe called again," Fatima said.

"That's good," Alex said. "Is she thinking of moving
home?"

"No, she just wanted to talk about plans for Chula's
birthday."

"Chula's birthday isn't until April, no?" Alex asked.

"I know," Fatima answered, "but Lupe's insane about it.
She's already saving up money."

"Is she going to invite your parents?" Alex asked.

"She said she wasn't, but she's inviting Eric's family. I
told her that by April, Mom and Dad would be over everything, but I don't think she believed me."

"Are your parents coming around?"

"I think my mom would if Lupe tried a little," Fatima said. "Mama loves babies and she misses Lupe. You can see it in her face when someone talks about Lupe. I don't know about my dad. He won't discuss her."

"He's just old-fashioned," Alex offered. "It was a big shock to him."

"Yeah, I guess. Lupe agreed to think about maybe talking to my mom sometime in the future." Fatima shrugged.

"That's progress," Alex said, and laughed. "Next time you talk to her, tell her I said hi, and I want to meet Chula."

"I will. Lupe did ask about you. She wanted to know if you were freaking out over that movie, *Iceman: The Beginning.*"

"I can't wait. It opens tomorrow," Alex gushed. "It's like I've been waiting for this movie to come out forever."

"I wasn't sure if you were still that into comic books anymore," Fatima said. Alex used to be crazy about Iceman. Back in middle school he had been obsessed. He even tried to make his own Iceman costume one Halloween.

"Of course I am."

Fatima picked up Carlos's book, ready to get back to work.

"How much longer are you going to do this guy's homework?" Alex asked.

"Tonight should be the last of it." Fatima wasn't sure if

she was happy about that or not. Once she stopped doing Carlos's homework she wouldn't have an excuse to talk to Carlos—or a reason to hang out at Alex's.

"Are you sure?"

"Yes. Their show's on Saturday at the White Rabbit, so he should have time to do his own homework again."

"After this we're free?"

"Yep." Fatima would be free to spend her evenings at water aerobics again. Great. "Let's finish this one," Fatima urged. "All we need to do is proofread it."

"Uh-huh." Alex scrolled through some of the paper, then looked at Fatima and said, "Nati refuses to go see another superhero movie. She claims she was traumatized by the last one. My dad can't really leave her alone, so I've got no one to go to the movie with."

"You want me to babysit? I don't mind. I really owe you." Alex and his dad did all sorts of stuff together. Fatima couldn't imagine her father taking her to the movies. A Spurs game, sure. Mr. Garcia knew someone who could get cheap tickets, and he would take the family sometimes. But take just Fatima to a movie? No way.

"Forget it," Alex said. He turned back to the computer.

"Forget what?"

"I was thinking we could celebrate the end of our homework indenture by going to the movie tomorrow."

"Together?" Fatima kind of liked the idea.

"Yes. Well, not together together. It doesn't have to be a

date or anything, just a celebration. I could go on my own, but I thought it might be more fun with you."

"Sure," Fatima said. "I've got nothing better to do, and it *might* be fun."

They didn't mention the "not date" again for the rest of the night.

The next day, Fatima pulled her hair into a haphazard ponytail as she rushed to the band parking lot for morning practice. The football players were always using the football field. The band had to make do with a parking lot with yard lines spray-painted on it. Fatima had two minutes to get there or else do push-ups. She could make it if she hurried.

"Hey," Carlos called.

She looked horrible in her plaid shorts and a faded oversized Spurs shirt. She felt dumpy and tired. She had already given him the homework, which was why she was now running late. She hadn't wanted to talk to him in her grungy practice clothes, so she had wasted precious minutes changing clothes after she'd talked to him.

Fatima reluctantly walked over to Carlos. There was no use hiding—he'd already seen her. "Did I forget something?" she asked.

"No, everything was perfect." Carlos grinned at her.

"Thanks, um, I really have to go," she said, ready to walk off.

"Wait. I don't wanna make you late, but you've been working so hard, I thought you deserved a night off." He leaned in closer to her. He smelled good. Exactly like a tall, sexy junior should smell.

"Night off?" she repeated stupidly.

"Yeah. I thought tonight I could take you somewhere to show my appreciation," he said.

"Tonight? Sure." Somewhere in the back of her mind she knew there was a reason she should say no. But with Carlos standing there, she couldn't think of a single thing more important than going out with him.

"I'll pick you up around six," he said. "Where do you live?"

In the distance, she heard the drum major calling the band to attention.

"Meet me at the corner of Kentucky and Elmendorf," she answered. He couldn't pick her up in front of her house. She didn't want him to see what a wreck she lived in, and there was no way her parents would ever let her get into a car with a boy.

"Okay. See you around six."

"Great."

Fatima floated to band practice. She was going out with Carlos Jones. The band secretary, an annoying clarinet, had seen Fatima talking to Carlos and seemed to take particular pleasure in making Fatima do push-ups for being late. Fatima didn't care. She could do a thousand push-ups and still be happy. Nothing could bring her down. Nothing, except seeing Alex. One look at him and everything slammed into her brain. What had she done?

"Alex will understand, right?" Fatima asked. Fatima, Vanna, and Olivia were gathered around a mirror in the restroom. Vanna was quickly putting on makeup, and Olivia was brushing her long hair. Athletes had locker rooms to change in and shower. Band members had to make do with restrooms. Band practice was always before school and during first period. There was never enough time to get ready for second period. The time constraint made things difficult, especially from August through October, when even the mornings were hot and humid in San Antonio. Everyone ended up sticky and smelly after practice. Fortunately, miracles *could* be worked with a little Noxzema and a lot of vanilla body spray.

Fatima, desperate for advice, had quickly filled Olivia and Vanna in on everything that had happened with Carlos and Alex.

"I don't think so. Guys are kinda funny about these things," Vanna said. She finished applying mascara, met Fatima's eyes in the mirror, and continued, "Alex has been giving up all his evenings to help you do some other guy's homework. Then you dump him? That's gonna hurt."

"You think I shouldn't go out with Carlos? But it's Carlos Jones! This is a once-in-a-lifetime opportunity. You understand, don't you, Olivia?"

"Yeah," Olivia said hesitantly, not looking at Fatima, "but it just doesn't seem like you to stand up a friend, even for Carlos. Besides, don't you think this is all happening kind of fast?"

"So?" Fatima said. "I am really not into questioning my good fortune. What's with you guys? I thought you'd be more excited."

"We are," Vanna replied. "It would have saved you a lot of trouble if you'd gotten Carlos to go out with you on a different day."

"Again. Gift horse, mouth, not looking and all that."

"I know," Vanna said, "but dumping Alex has gotta be bad for your karma."

"My grandma used to say," Olivia offered, *"Él que escupe por arriba—"*

"—se le cae encima," Fatima finished, and translated when Vanna looked puzzled, "He who spits up in the air has it land back on him."

"Ew, but I suppose it's accurate," Vanna said.

Fatima took a deep breath. "I know all this. I don't want to spit on Alex or hurt him. That's why I need you guys to help me figure out how to tell him."

"Would you rather go out with Carlos or Alex?" Olivia asked.

"Carlos," Fatima said. "I can go out with Alex anytime." She'd done all that homework so she could go out with Carlos, right?

"But if you choose Carlos over him, Alex is going to be

mad," Vanna pointed out. "I doubt he'd ask you out again after that."

"Think about it. Since you've known Alex, how many girls has he asked out?" Olivia asked.

"None as far as I know," Fatima said.

"Is Carlos worth possibly losing Alex as a friend?" Vanna asked.

"No." Fatima shook her head. "But Alex won't stay mad at me forever, will he?"

"Do you want to find out?" Olivia said. "Why don't you tell Carlos you changed your mind? It's not like he was ever your friend, so if he gets mad you won't be losing much."

"Please," Fatima said. "Like you would ever ditch Travis."

Olivia shrugged. Olivia had no idea what she would do in Fatima's situation. She'd probably never have two dates in one year, much less in one night.

"*Híjole*," Fatima said. What was with Vanna and Olivia? Were they her best friends or Alex's? "What if I want to take a gamble and do something crazy like go out with Carlos and postpone my thing with Alex? Y'all don't have any suggestions of what I should say to Alex?"

"Be honest. Alex will find out if you lie," was Vanna's advice.

"But be vague," Olivia said. "It might be easier on him. He doesn't have to know why. Just that you can't make it."

"Tell him soon and get it over with," Vanna added.

"And in a crowded place like the cafeteria. He's less likely to cause a scene."

"You really think he's gonna be mad enough to cause a scene?" Fatima asked.

"You never know," Vanna said.

Olivia offered a hopeful smile and wished her luck.

"Thanks, that's a lot of help," Fatima mumbled as she headed to U.S. history.

16

Fatima decided to take Vanna's advice and talk to Alex in the cafeteria. She tracked him down as soon as the bell rang for lunch.

"Can I talk to you?" she asked. They were surrounded by students, making it a very public place. Everyone around them was so absorbed in their own conversations that no one paid any attention to Fatima and Alex, guaranteeing them privacy.

"Sure, I guess," he said.

"About tonight," she said, taking a deep breath. "I think we're going to have to postpone it."

"What? Why? Did something happen?"

"No, well . . . something came up that I have to do."

"Something just . . ." Alex trailed off. "It's him, isn't it? He snapped his fingers, and you jumped! What is it now? Are you washing his car for him?"

"It's not like that. He's taking me out—"

"You feel it's okay to ditch me, now that something better has come along?"

"No, I—"

"That's not right, Fatima. I thought you were smart, but you're an idiot. You're letting him control you." Alex was angry. And he had a point, but Fatima really wanted to go out with Carlos.

"He's not controlling me!" she protested. She could kick herself for telling Alex. "I can make this up to you, I promise," she mumbled weakly.

"How could I not have seen this coming? I really thought we . . . never mind."

"No, you're getting it all wrong. We are cool together. And I was looking forward to the movie. But . . . you have to understand, this is Carlos we're talking about." This wasn't going well at all. Nothing wonderful ever happened to Fatima, and now Alex was ruining it for her.

"Yeah, Carlos is hot, and I'm . . . not. I get it," Alex said, starting to walk away.

"I know how this sounds, and I'm sorry." Fatima grabbed his arm.

"That's great. Now just leave me alone." He tried to wiggle out of her grasp.

But she wouldn't let go. Years of hanging on to squirmy younger siblings enabled her to keep him trapped. If only he wouldn't be mad, then everything would be all right.

"What's it gonna take for you to get over this?" she said.

"Get over this? Someone thinks highly of herself. Don't worry, I think I'll manage."

"I know I owe you, so—"

"Do you really think I'm so desperate that I have to trick girls into dating me? I had no idea I was that pathetic," Alex interrupted.

Fatima felt awful. He looked hurt. She'd hurt him.

"You're not pathetic. You're . . ." she hesitated. She didn't want to say the wrong thing and upset him further. "A good friend" didn't seem appropriate. "Kind of cute" didn't sound right either. Funny? He was occasionally funny.

"Not Carlos," he finished for her. "We keep coming back to that."

"You're funny," she said hopefully.

He gave her a look of exasperated astonishment, and coldly said, "Get your hands off of me. I can't stand the sight of you right now."

She jerked back as if she'd been slapped and let go of him. He had never talked to her like that before.

"What's your deal, Alex? Just because we have to put off our celebration doesn't mean it's the end of the world! Why can't you understand how much this means to me? Why can't you be at least a little happy for me?"

"Oh, but I am," he said with a sneer. "Can't you see? I'm overjoyed. I hope you have a great time with your dream boy. You two are perfect for each other." He shook his head in disgust and stormed off.

"Alex!" she yelled after him, but he kept walking. "Alex! Come back here! I'm not finished."

"Alex," she said softly, "I'm sorry. I really didn't mean to hurt you."

Fatima was hot and hungry. She'd never felt more fat or awkward in her life. She sat in a stuffy, dimly lit garage on a raggedy blue loveseat. Her fingers traced the clusters of small burn holes where dozens of cigarettes had been snuffed out. She was the only girl sweating. She was totally overdressed in her red, long-sleeved boatneck blouse and black pants.

Fatima shared the loveseat with Miranda, a super-skinny girl in hip-hugger jeans and a camouflage tank top. Fatima took up twice as much space as Miranda did. She was surrounded by tiny girls in spaghetti-strap tops and shorts. One girl sat in a corner wearing an ankle-length black skirt and a long-sleeved black shirt with white makeup caked on her face. That girl should have been sweating off all her black eye makeup, but she looked as cool as could be. Fatima could have been sitting in an air-conditioned movie theater eating butter-drenched popcorn with Alex. But the popcorn would have only made her gain weight. She was probably better off sweating.

This was her grand date with Carlos Jones—watching his band practice. Pulgas. Fleas. They seemed aptly named since the loveseat she was sitting on was full of fleas. Every flea must have bitten her at least twice. Fleas draw out a fraction of an ounce of blood with every bite. Maybe if enough bit Fatima, she'd lose a pound.

She could endure this minor torture for Carlos. Not that he'd really even spoken to her. He had shown up late with a van full of people and told her to "hop in," then had driven over to someone's garage.

The band was playing some punk-sounding song, which involved a great deal of yelling. Carlos was actually a pretty decent drummer. He was good enough for marching band, she thought as she watched him. He'd worked up a sexy sheen of sweat, but he still pounded away. Fatima wondered if Alex had found someone else to take to the movies.

Someone handed Miranda a joint, and she took a deep puff.

"Hey, you want some?" she offered Fatima.

Fatima froze. She had never smoked pot and didn't want to. But she didn't want to seem like a goody-goody.

"So, you want some or what?" Miranda said, waving the joint.

"What? Oh, I couldn't hear you. The music's too loud. No, not right now. I'm good," Fatima said. She hoped she sounded casual.

"Whatever," Miranda said, turning back to the band.

What? No ridicule? No after-school-special-ish jeering? She should have known these people were too cool to care what a freshman did.

Practice continued for about an hour. Then someone's mother came in and said the neighbors were complaining about the noise. That was the end of practice. The band left, including Carlos.

Fatima sat next to Miranda, who looked pleasantly spacey, wondering what to do next. Was Carlos going to leave her there? She didn't even know whose garage this was. She could only imagine what her mother would say if she called her and told her she didn't know where she was and didn't have a way to get home. Her mother thought she was at Vanna's house studying for an English test.

"Where'd the guys go?" she asked Miranda.

"The band?"

"Yeah."

"Oh, Jay probably had some stuff. Don't you worry your pretty little head about it," Miranda said, patting Fatima's knee. "They'll be back soon, better than ever." She leaned back in the loveseat and gave in to fits of giggling.

Okay, weirdo, Fatima thought. That really helped a lot. Her mind drifted back to Alex. Had he gone to the movie? Alone? Or maybe he'd found someone better than her to go with.

"Miranda Bananda," Jay, the lead singer, said from the doorway as the rest of the band filtered in. He tilted his head as he waited for Miranda to respond.

"Bananda. He's such an idiot," Miranda said, laughing. She sauntered over to him and leaped on his back, wrapping her legs around his waist and her arms around his neck.

"Hey, Fatty," Carlos yelled from across the room.

Please, don't let him be talking to me, Fatima prayed.

"Fatty, we gotta get going," he said, looking directly at her. In an effort to minimize the embarrassment, Fatima jumped up and rushed over to him, ignoring the giggles. At least he hadn't forgotten her.

"There's some new comic book movie opening today. It's supposed to have a killer soundtrack. I thought we'd go check it out," he said.

Fatima was going to see *Iceman* after all, but with Carlos. They would share a soda, and hopefully a large tub of popcorn. She was starving. Would Alex be there? It was possible, but Fatima doubted it. Alex had probably gone to the first showing right after school.

Carlos didn't wait for an answer. He headed for his car without looking back. She followed, watching him, and climbed into the front seat of the van. She had hoped she would get to ride in his Nissan Z. She didn't know who this ugly van belonged to. She had never seen him drive it before.

Carlos dominated the conversation the whole way to River Center Mall. He didn't give her a chance to speak.

"What didya think? We were great, huh? I mean, we've only been together a year or so, but I think we've got it. We're gonna be the next Nirvana, you know? But I think our name's gonna hold us back. Pulgas. It sounds so Mexican, like a Tejano band. That's not what we're about. But Martin thinks it'll make us stand out. Martin's got connections. He got us the gig at the White Rabbit. We're gonna be seen. Discovered. Signed. We're gonna be the next Nirvana, man!" He babbled. Some of what he said didn't even make sense, and he kept repeating himself.

Fatima didn't mind. This was the most he'd ever said to her.

Fatima recognized the girl behind the ticket counter. Fatima sat next to her in math class, but had never spoken to her before.

"Hey, Mel, can you hook me up with some *Iceman* tickets?" Carlos said, leaning on the counter.

"Sorry, Carlos, I can't. The manager's watching us carefully," she said. She flashed him a metallic smile.

"C'mon, Mel."

"Really, I can't. I'll lose my job."

"That's cool. Well, I haven't got the cash on me. Fatty, can you get us two tickets?" he said. He stepped out of the way so she could get to the counter.

This shouldn't disappoint me, Fatima thought as she handed over the cash. It isn't the 1950s. Guys shouldn't be expected to pay for everything. However, she had to use all her cash for the tickets, so there would be no money for popcorn. Her stomach growled in protest.

She should have eaten at home, but she had foolishly assumed they would go someplace for a romantic dinner. She hadn't wanted to waste her calories eating at home if she was just going to eat again. In fact, she hadn't eaten much that day. She had been too nervous about the date.

By the time they found the theater, the movie had already started. Carlos led her to the front row.

"Don't you want to try for something farther back? It's hard to see from here," Fatima whispered.

"It doesn't matter. I don't care about the stupid movie. I just want to hear the music," Carlos said a little too loudly. A few people shushed him.

Fatima shocked herself by enjoying the movie. With a name like *Iceman*, she hadn't expected much. It would have been nice to watch the movie with someone who had read the comic books and knew the backstory. Someone like Alex. For as much as Carlos talked about the music, he sure didn't sit through much of the movie. He kept leaving to go to the bathroom or get a drink of water. Fatima could take a hint. Either he was worried about being seen with her, or he just plain couldn't stand being near her. She suddenly felt exhausted and was starving, and she wanted this nightmare of a date over with.

As soon as the credits started rolling, she left the theater to wait for Carlos in the lobby. Perhaps it had been the blasting music at Carlos's practice, or too much time spent cooped up with the pot fumes in the overheated garage, or simple starvation, but something had given Fatima a diabolical headache. The kind of headache that turned your stomach and burned your eyes. No matter how good-looking Carlos was, he wasn't worth this aggravation.

"So what do you wanna do now?" Carlos asked when he returned from his twentieth visit to the bathroom.

"I want to go home," she said as she looked at him. He was sort of dancing from foot to foot. His eyes were dilated, and he was sweating even as Fatima shivered in the air-conditioning.

"Fine. Let's go. Do you remember where we parked?" he said, walking off again and clearly expecting her to follow. But her feet wouldn't move. An overwhelming foreboding coursed through her. She could not get into that van with him.

"No," she said. "I'm not coming with you."

"What?" He turned around in confusion and stared at her.

"I want to go home, but not with you," she said. Suddenly, it all made sense. The sweating, the trips to the bathroom, the jitteriness, and the dilated eyes. It was more than just pot. She'd seen the symptoms before on one of those cheesy videos in health class. "You're on something, *baboso*!"

He didn't bother to deny it.

"How dare you? *Estupido!* You could have killed me." The Spanish she worked so hard not to use always slipped back in when she was upset.

"Look, it's no big deal. I know when I'm okay to drive. Chill, all right?"

"*Pendejo!* You don't know anything. *Vete!* Just go away and leave me alone. And get someone else to do your homework. I quit!" Fatima couldn't believe her own ears. After all, she should be grateful that Carlos had gone out with her. She was just a chubby freshman, and he was . . . a mess. She had worked hard to get this date. Too hard. She had sold out her brain for this?

"Fine! Your loss!" He stomped away without giving her a second glance.

"No, yours," she whispered.

Fatima slumped on a bench outside the mall. She was quickly beginning to realize that dumping him, though it made her feel vindicated, had also stranded her. What good was her righteous woman power going to do her when she called her mother? She wouldn't cry. Crying wouldn't help anything.

"Fatima?" a familiar voice called out.

"Great. Just when I thought things couldn't get any worse," she mumbled. Out of all the theaters in San Antonio, he would have to show up here. "Look, Alex, I know I was a jerk to you. I was inexcusably horrible, and wouldn't blame you if you never spoke to me again. Don't worry, I've been punished, okay? I couldn't possibly feel any worse. So, please, please, *dejame en paz*. Leave me alone."

Alex sat down next to her.

"I heard your conversation with Carlos. I didn't mean to eavesdrop, but you were kinda loud," he said, smiling slightly.

All of a sudden she couldn't hold it back anymore. A wave of tears burst out of her.

"It was awful! I'm stranded and hungry. I couldn't eat now if I wanted to. It's after nine o'clock. Anything you eat after nine turns into fat. I'm covered in flea bites. I have no money and . . . I SMELL LIKE POT!" she wailed. People milling around the mall entrance stared at her. "I don't know what to do! I never know what to do."

"Shh, it's okay. It's not the end of the world," he said, patting her back.

"It feels like it is." She sniffed and struggled to regain her composure.

"If you had gone home with him, that would have been profoundly stupid. Sometimes you're smarter than I give you credit for."

"Gee, thanks." Fatima could almost feel herself smiling.

"You have to admit, you went all girlie stupid for that *payaso*," Alex said. Fatima had never heard anyone refer to Carlos as a clown.

"Oh, don't remind me. I still have no idea what I'm going to do right now."

"I'll buy you some pizza. And don't worry about your carbs. If you don't eat, your body will go into starvation mode and store twice as much fat on the next thing you eat, no matter what time it is. My dad's picking me up, and I know he won't mind giving you a ride home."

"What about the pot? My mom will kill me."

"Don't worry. I don't have to call my dad right away.

After we eat, we'll stroll through CVS. You can test out a few different perfumes. As for the flea bites, which I don't even want to ask about, I can't do much about them, but I promise I won't think badly if you scratch 'em. Cool?"

"Yeah, I guess," she said. Suddenly, Alex didn't seem quite so stupid. Not exactly a knight in shining armor, but close.

"We've got some time before my dad comes. Let's go for a walk," Alex said after they'd eaten. "It's actually decent out for a change. We must be getting a cold front or something." He gathered up their trash and placed it on his tray. No one ever cleaned up after her. Fatima was the one forever picking up after, feeding, or bathing some sibling.

"Sure," she managed to say, following him. "I've always liked the river at night." She'd been to the River Walk only to watch parades with her family, but Fatima never enjoyed herself. She was usually too busy making sure Juan or Diego didn't fall or throw something in the river or try to steal something from the street vendors. Or she was too tired from sitting out in the sun (one of her most favorite things to do) saving their parade-watching spot. The parades were free, but the good spots filled up fast. The worst time had been for the Spurs' NBA championship parade. Her family had to set up at nine in the morning for a parade that started at six in the evening.

"Hard to believe this same river runs all the way to our school. Of course it's not half as pretty by the time it gets to us," Alex said. "Our river only has weeds."

Fatima and Alex walked in silence down the River Walk, the bread and butter of San Antonio tourism. People came for the Alamo and stayed to party on the river. Fatima and Alex waved at the tourists as they rode past on barges and eyed the food of the people dining on the patios of expensive restaurants. Pulsing music leaked out of a club, mixing with raucous singing from an Irish pub farther down the river. Fatima was getting her romantic stroll in the moonlight after all. The only thing missing was mariachis.

Fatima couldn't enjoy herself, not until she cleared everything up with Alex. So she took a deep breath and said, "I still owe you a date."

"Forget about it," Alex said.

"I don't want to forget it," she said and sighed. "It's not like I didn't want to go out with you."

"You just wanted to go out with Carlos more."

"I thought that's what I wanted," Fatima said. "I made the wrong decision, and I'm sorry."

Alex shrugged.

A girl can apologize only so much. "Look, homecoming's coming up. We could go to that."

Alex turned and looked at her.

Fatima went on nervously, "I couldn't actually go with you. My parents would never allow that thanks to Lupe, but I could meet you there, and, um"—she paused to wet her lips—"we could hang out."

17

"Any human being would at least pretend to care about his daughter on her birthday," Vanna said. "My father must not be human. He still hasn't called."

"No card or anything?" Alex asked. He turned around in his seat to face them.

"Nope," Vanna said. "Watch out for my trombone."

"Maybe he's just late," Olivia offered.

"It's already been three days."

They were on a school bus headed for the last Saturday game of the season. Alex had their instruments piled next to him and was talking to Vanna and Olivia. Low brass, drumline, and saxophones shared a bus whenever the whole band went anywhere. Since those were pretty small sections, they always had plenty of space, so overflow from the other buses also rode with them. Fatima and Alex usually rode with them because there was never enough room on the flute/clarinet bus or the trumpet/French horn bus. But today Fatima didn't. The day Olivia wanted badly to talk to her, Fatima decided not to ride with them.

"So, what did you do last night?" Olivia asked Vanna. "Sorry I couldn't come over to watch *Buffy* with you."

"You didn't miss much," Vanna said. "My mom was going to join my marathon, but by the third episode, her boyfriend had called so many times I told her to just go out with him."

"That stinks," Alex said.

"It's not a big deal." Vanna shrugged, though of course she did think it was a big deal. It would be nice if her mother showed an interest in spending time with her. "What's up with Fatima?"

"Did she tell you anything?" Olivia asked Alex.

"Um . . . not exactly."

"What did she tell you?" Vanna demanded.

"She didn't have to tell me. I was there."

"What?" Vanna and Olivia both exclaimed.

"She and Carlos went to the same movie she and I were supposed to go to."

"Ouch." Vanna wondered what Fatima had been thinking. Picking Carlos over Alex was one thing. Why rub his face in it?

"And you ran into them?" Olivia asked. Fatima's love life was like a soap opera.

"Sorta," Alex said. "Apparently she and Carlos had a really bad date. You'll have to get the details from her. They ended up yelling at each other outside the theater."

"Fatima yelled at Carlos Jones?" Vanna couldn't believe it.

"That's awful," Olivia added.

Alex nodded. "Anyway, Fatima and I ended up hanging out."

"And?" Vanna prompted. Now things were really getting interesting.

"And, we're going to the homecoming dance together."

"Ha!" Vanna barked, turning to Olivia. "Told you."

"How did you know?" Olivia asked. Would she ever understand relationships the way Vanna did?

"Classic Xander and Cordelia—*Buffy* season two," Vanna replied.

"What?" Olivia was confused. She'd never actually watched *Buffy*.

"You watch way too much TV," Alex said.

Vanna ignored him, and continued, "It's the whole 'let's act like we hate each other, then go make out in a broom closet' syndrome."

"We didn't make out or anything," Alex said.

"Whatever, you get my point."

"So, how long have you liked her?" Olivia asked. Why hadn't she noticed? Olivia had known Alex and Fatima forever.

Alex sighed. "Y'all can't tell Fatima any of this. It'll freak her out."

"Fine, fine. We won't," Vanna agreed. "Now tell us."

"Since third grade."

"That's when you put a roach in her hair," Olivia said. "You traumatized her for life." Olivia had seen Fatima take snails, lizards, crickets, and all sorts of creepy crawlies away from her little brothers with her bare hands. Fatima would kill a fly or spider without flinching, but ever since the roach incident in third grade she hadn't been able to face cockroaches.

"I know," Alex said. "It was not the smoothest move."

Olivia counted on her fingers. "That's almost seven years, and you make fun of me and Travis. I've only liked him for three years."

"The difference is that I'm friends with her," Alex said. "She never really showed any interest in guys, so I just kinda waited for the right moment. Then all of a sudden she goes out with Carlos the moron. I should have been the guy she went out with, not him. Carlos can't appreciate her. I . . ."

"You what?" Vanna asked.

"You like her?" Olivia offered.

"It's lasted since third grade. I think it's a little stronger than like," Alex answered.

"You love her!" Vanna squealed. This was way better than a TV show.

"I, um, I don't know about that." He took a deep breath. *"La quiero."*

"You want her?" Olivia gasped.

"Ew," Vanna said. "Way too much information."

"Honestly, Olivia, aren't you part Mexican?" Alex asked.

"Quiero means 'want,' right?" Olivia countered. People always challenged her Hispanicness. Why couldn't her dad's last name have been Sanchez? Then no one would question Olivia's ethnicity no matter how white she looked. Life would have been easier.

"When you say it in Spanish, it means that you really feel something for a person. More than like, but maybe not quite love," Alex explained.

"Oh," Olivia said. She would just about die if any guy ever wanted her like that.

"Now, you can't tell Fatima this. Things are weird enough as it is," he said as the bus came to a stop in front of Alamo Stadium. "My only question is, how does she feel about me?"

Olivia and Vanna were saved from answering that question by the section leaders yelling for everyone to hurry and line up.

Olivia rushed out of the bus and scrambled into line before the drum major called them to attention, wondering the same thing as Alex. She had no idea how her supposed best friend felt, but she intended to find out.

18

Olivia felt the usual blast of excitement as the band entered the stadium. Alamo Stadium, located across from Trinity University on a "nice" side of town, was where all the inner-city schools had their sporting events. It was an old stadium that had been built in the thirties by the WPA. It wasn't a huge state-of-the-art facility like the northside schools had, but in Olivia's opinion, with its beautiful stonework and Art Deco lettering, it was way cooler.

Every time Olivia marched in it, she felt important, like the crowd in the stands was there to see her. Of course, afternoon games weren't like night games. Night games had the bright lights and bigger crowds. This afternoon, Olivia was determined to talk to Fatima. She just had to wait for the right moment.

The right moment came at the end of the third quarter. The brass and drumline started playing a pep cheer. The rest of the band danced. Fatima hadn't come to Olivia's section to talk after halftime, so Olivia snuck down to the flutes while everyone was distracted. She intended to grill Fatima about her date, but took one look at her and changed her mind. Fatima looked pale and tired.

"Are you all right?" Olivia asked.

"What are you doing?" Fatima was shocked. Olivia was out of her section without permission? "You're gonna get in trouble."

"I know," Olivia said, for once not caring about the threat of push-ups. "What's going on?"

"Did Alex tell you about yesterday?"

"Um, yeah." Olivia chose her words carefully. She had promised Alex that she wouldn't tell Fatima how he felt about her. She wouldn't, but she wasn't going to lie to her best friend either. "He told us about you two."

"Really?"

"Yeah. So, how do you feel about him?"

"I, well, I—" Fatima began.

At that moment, the football team decided to score. They hadn't scored all game, but that was just Olivia's luck. The drum major called them to attention. Olivia rushed back to her section and launched into the school fight song. Olivia didn't get another chance to talk to Fatima for the rest of the game because the football team kept scoring. They ended up winning.

After the game, figuring desperate times called for desperate measures, Olivia snuck onto the flute/clarinet bus.

She squeezed into a seat in the back next to a surprised Fatima.

"I know I'm living dangerously, but we have to talk," Olivia said.

"Well, at least sit next to the window," Fatima said, getting up, "so no one notices your saxophone."

"Good idea." Olivia scooted over. "What is going on with you and Alex? I know something's up, so you might as well spill."

Fatima sighed. It would have been easier opening up on the phone, but at her house she'd never find the privacy. Her parents would flip if they got the slightest inkling that something might be going on between Fatima and a boy. So the back of the bus in the fading afternoon light among about fifty cheering woodwinds would have to do.

"Alex has been my friend forever," Fatima finally said.

Olivia had technically been Fatima's friend longer, but she didn't point that out. "And you don't want to mess up the friendship?"

"It's not that . . ." Fatima searched for the right words. How could she explain something she didn't really understand herself?

"What?" Olivia asked.

"I don't belong with him."

"Huh?" Olivia looked confused. "You belong with Carlos?"

"No," Fatima replied.

"Is there someone else?" How could Olivia not have realized Fatima liked someone else? Did she know Fatima at all anymore?

"No." Fatima looked away.

Olivia tried again. "I understand the whole belonging thing. I belong with Travis. I know it in my being. It's like I can't see any other guy that way."

"What if he never sees you that way?"

"I don't know. I've tried to give up on him and move on, but you know I can't," Olivia said.

"I don't feel that way about Alex," Fatima said. "I never thought of him as a guy guy until recently."

"And?"

"And he is smart, sorta cute, and, aside from his occasional bouts of annoyingness, pretty cool. But he's Alex."

"So you just don't like Alex?" This was what Olivia had been worried about. If Fatima broke Alex's heart, things would be weird.

"No. That's not what I'm saying." Fatima didn't know what she was saying, truth be told.

"Fatima, you're not making sense," Olivia said, now thoroughly lost.

"I know."

"You always make sense."

"I know."

That seemed to be the end of that, Olivia thought as she watched the city go by outside the bus window. The farther the bus got from the stadium, the smaller and more run-down the houses appeared. She spotted the old Pearl Brewery, where a lot of kids' parents used to work before it was shut down. Luckily, Toyota had opened a factory way on the south side of town, so most of the people who had been laid off from various plant closings had gotten jobs there.

"He's too skinny," Fatima burst out. She had been thinking about this since the previous night, and everything boiled down to that.

"What?" Olivia asked.

"He's too skinny. How would it look if we started walking around holding hands and stuff?"

"Fine?" Olivia offered.

"No, we'd look like Jack Sprat and his fat wife."

"Jack . . . huh?" Olivia tried to remember the nursery rhyme.

"A thin guy and a tub of lard," Fatima explained.

"Wait a minute," Olivia said. "First of all, you are no tub of lard." She swatted Fatima for emphasis. "Secondly, why are you even worried about that? You didn't seem to care with Carlos."

"Carlos was like playing the lottery. In the back of my mind, I knew nothing would ever happen, but I had to try anyway. Alex is different. He's a good guy and he likes me. The guys tease him enough as it is. Can you imagine if he started dating a fat girl? He doesn't deserve that."

"I think Alex can take care of himself. If what the guys thought was going to be a problem for him, he wouldn't have said he'd go to the dance with you."

"He hasn't thought about it yet. But once he realizes . . ."

Fatima said. She looked at Olivia, and Olivia could see the pain in Fatima's eyes. "I don't want him to realize."

This was not Fatima. Fatima didn't care what other people thought. Olivia put her arm around Fatima. "Are you listening to yourself? Do you know what you're saying?"

Fatima nodded.

"You're saying that you, Fatima Garcia, beautiful, strong, math genius extraordinaire, aren't good enough for Alex."

"I'm not . . ." Fatima started to protest.

"Because you're not a size four, you can't have a boyfriend?" Olivia challenged.

"You don't understand." Fatima shrugged off Olivia's arm. "If you and Travis ever got together, you guys would look great. You're both tall and thin."

Olivia took a deep breath, then said, "How many times have you listened to me whine about not being good enough for Travis?"

"Too many."

"And you always convince me that I am. What do you say?"

Fatima was silent.

"You tell me that I'm smart and sweet and he would be lucky to have me," Olivia answered.

"So?"

"So you never mention my weight. Why is your weight so important?"

"It's different. You can't understand." Fatima couldn't possibly explain to skinny, cute Olivia what being chubby and plain was like.

"Maybe I can't," Olivia said as the bus turned down the street in front of their school. "All I know is Alex likes you. Really, really likes you. Not you ten pounds lighter or you without glasses. But you, right now, exactly as you are. If you don't like him, there might be a problem. But you do like him. Do you know how lucky you are to like a boy that likes you back? I've been waiting three years for Travis. You have Alex, and you're letting what other people, who you don't know, might possibly think get in the way. That makes absolutely no sense."

"Well, when you put it that way."

"Maybe you're scared or something. I don't know. But you need to talk to Alex."

When Fatima started to say something, Olivia held up her hand and said, "Talk to Alex, and give him a chance. Don't hide behind your weight. Either go out with him or don't, based on how you feel about him, not on how you feel about yourself."

The bus came to a stop and people started exiting.

"When did you get so wise?" Fatima smiled at her best friend.

"I do think of things other than Travis occasionally," Olivia said, and laughed.

"You know what?"

"Hmmm?" Olivia said, gathering up her hat, instrument, gloves, and sheet music.

"You should really take your own advice."

"What?"

"Stop being scared of what Travis might think of you, and just talk to him."

19

After the game, Vanna finished watching season three of *Buffy the Vampire Slayer*, including the extras, by herself. Fatima and Olivia were busy with their families, and Vanna's mother had a date. Vanna still couldn't believe her dad hadn't called. He had never forgotten her birthday before. Not that she wanted to talk to him. But even her grandma had sent a card with twenty bucks.

By Sunday afternoon, she was sick of thinking about her father.

"I'm back," she shouted on her way to the kitchenette. She set a plastic drugstore bag on the counter and fished out a bottle of ibuprofen.

Her mother had snuck in at six o'clock that morning. Vanna had heard her slam the front door. At two o'clock, her mom had complained of a headache. Of course, they were out of pain relievers, so when Vanna couldn't take any more nagging, she'd walked the six blocks to the drugstore to buy some.

"Thank you," her mother said. She was wearing a long purple terry-cloth robe, her hair wrapped in a pink towel.

Vanna stuffed the unopened bottle into her mother's hands. "I couldn't figure out the childproof cap."

"You are such a good daughter. Taking care of me."

"What can I say? You need me," Vanna said. She filled a glass with tap water and handed it to her mom. "I'm glad to see you felt good enough to take a shower. Being clean always makes a person feel better."

"Truth is I was planning on lying around in my pajamas and vegging with you, but"—she shot Vanna an embarrassed smile—"Bob called. He says he can't bear to be apart from me today. He threatened to come over and take care of me. I can't have him seeing this mess."

Or me, Vanna thought. "You're going out tonight? I thought you were on the verge of death."

"I was, and still am a little. But you were right about the shower, and after some makeup, I'll be good to go."

"Do you really need to go out on a Sunday night?" Vanna asked.

"We're just getting coffee. I won't be out late. You know, Bob's wasn't the only phone call I got while you were out."

"Hmmm," Vanna mumbled. Another evening with the TV for company. She wondered if an inanimate object, such as a television set, could be considered a best friend.

"That woman called," her mom said, rubbing her hair with the towel.

"What woman?"

"Your father's mother. She says she has to see you this afternoon. I told her you'd call her." Mrs. Reynolds paused and tried to shake some water out of her ear. "Now, don't make that face."

Vanna rolled her eyes, heaved a heavy sigh, then began, "But—"

"I know she and I don't get along. I'm shocked I made it through a five-minute phone conversation with her." Her mom pulled a nail file out of her robe pocket. "But she's the only grandparent you've got. You should try and connect with her."

"Easier said than done." It wasn't that Vanna hated her grandmother. She didn't know her well enough to hate her. Vanna typically saw her grandmother twice a year: Thanksgiving and Christmas. She would much rather spend Sunday afternoon curled up on the couch with some popcorn and a movie than make stilted conversation with an old lady who never seemed to be pleased.

"Try," her mother said without looking up from her nails.

"I'll call her later." By "later," Vanna meant never.

"Don't be a wimp. Do it now."

"We've been living in San Antonio for months. Why does she suddenly have to see me now?" Vanna asked.

"Who knows? Maybe she thinks she's gonna die or something."

"Mom!"

"Don't worry," her mother continued, "the old harpy will probably outlive us all. I told her you'd be there, so just go for a few minutes. And be polite. Make sure to thank her for the money she sent you. I don't want her to think I'm raising a heathen or anything. Okay?"

When Vanna didn't immediately grab the phone, Mrs. Reynolds said, "Look, you'll never know what's going on until you call her. Your grandma and your dad aren't that bad. Just give them a chance."

Them? How had her father gotten into the conversation?

"Oh, and the car's out of gas so it would be great if you could get her to pick you up or take the bus there." Her mom tossed her the phone and left the room.

Vanna couldn't help but feel that her mom's dating life always came at Vanna's expense. Would it have killed her to put off the date for an hour or so and go with her for moral support, even if she just waited in the car? She was Vanna's mother after all.

Vanna sighed and dialed the phone. Grandma Reynolds picked up after one ring.

"My mom said you wanted to see me today?"

"Yes, Vanessa, as soon as possible," Grandma Reynolds answered.

"Is everything okay?" Something could have happened

to Vanna's father. That sick feeling she had felt after talking to Olivia about dead fathers crept into her stomach.

"Everything's fine. There are some matters I wish to discuss with you."

"Matters?" Vanna asked. Why all the secrecy?

"Yes, Vanessa, matters that concern you." Impatience tinged Grandma Reynolds's voice. "I'll expect you within the hour."

Vanna was about to say, "Well, you can expect all you want. I'm not going anywhere," but her mother walked by and mouthed, "Be nice." So Vanna asked, "Can you pick me up?"

"I'm afraid not. My car is in the shop at the moment."

"I guess I'll take the bus." Vanna sighed again.

"Lovely, see you soon," Mrs. Reynolds said, and that was the end of the conversation.

Getting ready didn't take too long. She wasn't worried about impressing her grandmother. Vanna brushed her teeth and put on some makeup. She went heavy on the eyeliner. Grandma always hated that.

"Ma," she said, poking her head into her mother's room. Her mom was drying her hair. Vanna had to yell a few times to get her attention.

"Leaving already?" Her mom turned off the blow-dryer.

"Yeah, I might as well get it over with." Wow, Vanna couldn't help thinking, her mom was a knockout. Purely gorgeous. Her perfectly shiny shoulder-length blond hair never seemed to frizz. She knew exactly how to accent her huge green eyes and amazing body. Why didn't I inherit any of that? Vanna thought, feeling very redheaded and ugly.

"I'll have my phone. Call me if you need anything, okay?" Mrs. Reynolds said. Vanna noticed she had an odd, sad look in her eyes.

"Are you all right?"

"Oh, yeah. Just nervous I guess." Her mother blinked and the look was gone. She smiled.

Nervous about a coffee date? Her mom was getting weirder and weirder. "About going out with Bob? You just saw him."

"No, no." Ms. Reynolds paused. "I just want you to know that you're not alone. I'm here if you need me."

"Okay," Vanna said suspiciously. What was going on?

"Well, good luck. Give me a kiss."

Vanna gave her mom a kiss on the cheek. Mmm, she's wearing the pumpkin pie scent, Vanna thought.

"You smell good," Vanna said. Whatever was going on, her mother obviously didn't want to talk about it.

"Good enough to eat, right?" Her mother giggled.

"I guess so."

"Here. Have some," her mother said. She picked up the perfume and spritzed Vanna a few times. "You probably smell like that couch you've been living on."

"Thanks a lot," Vanna mumbled as she left the room.

20

A cool breeze tossed Vanna's curls around as she walked from the bus stop to her grandma's house. San Antonio was finally starting to cool off. Everyone said it wouldn't last— winter didn't really hit San Antonio until January. And by March, it would be hot again.

Her grandmother probably knew why her father hadn't called on Vanna's birthday. Maybe he was going to marry his girlfriend and he was making Grandma break the news to Vanna.

"Thanks for remembering my birthday," Vanna said when her grandmother answered the door.

"You're welcome. How was it?" Grandma Reynolds asked.

They chatted about the Chart House as Vanna followed her to the kitchen. Vanna stopped cold when she saw her father sitting at the table.

"What are you doing here?" Vanna demanded.

"I wanted to talk to you, and I knew you wouldn't see me if I asked," he answered.

"So you tricked me?"

"I suppose, but I miss you."

"You miss me!"

"I know things haven't been great between us, but—"

"Great between us?" Vanna said. "You gave up on us, on me. You didn't love me enough to stay with Mom. Well, you missed your chance to be my father."

Vanna grabbed her jacket from her grandmother with a flourish. She'd told her father off and was headed for the perfect dramatic exit. But he wasn't playing along. He was supposed to yell back. Instead, he was just sitting in his chair staring at her. He looked tired and much older than she remembered. His light brown hair had more gray. His stomach strained the buttons on his white shirt.

She wouldn't let herself feel sorry for him. He had nearly destroyed her mother, and now he wanted to destroy Vanna, too. She didn't need him.

"I don't know what you hoped to accomplish with this little stunt," she said. Her grandmother was surprisingly quiet. Even so, Vanna was prepared to fight them both. She jammed her arms into the sleeves of her jacket. "This was a waste of my time." She turned and walked out of the kitchen toward the living room.

"We were miserable, you know," Mr. Reynolds said.

Vanna heard his chair scraping the tile. I should keep walking, she thought.

"I was making her so unhappy. And the fighting all the time had to have affected you."

She stopped where she was, but didn't turn to face him. She couldn't resist saying, "Not more than your cheating, Dad. When I woke up one morning and had to move to a disgusting apartment and leave all my friends, I was affected. When I listened to Mom cry every night, I was pretty darn affected."

"She's better off now. I was stifling her. But you . . . You're in so much pain it kills me."

She turned to him with a bitter smile and said, "Good," then headed to the living room with the intention of storming out of the house. Her father didn't follow, but her grandmother did.

"Vanessa, may I show you something?"

Vanna sighed. "Grandma, not now. Getting tricked puts me in a bad mood."

"Vanna, please."

Vanna's grandmother was carrying an old photo album. Huh? She wants to show me pictures now? Vanna thought. The old lady must really be losing it.

Curiosity made Vanna sit down on the couch next to her grandmother.

Inside the album were black-and-white pictures of high school students. In some of the pictures the kids wore band uniforms. Uncomfortable-looking uniforms with ruffled collars.

"I don't suppose you recognize the place," Grandma Reynolds said.

"Um, no. Should I?"

"That's Hamilton High School, and that's me."

"You were in band? You went to Hamilton?" Vanna couldn't imagine her prim and proper grandmother going to school in a place like Hamilton. She seemed more the boarding school type.

"It was different back then," Grandma Reynolds said. "We were the best. None of this fourth-place business."

Vanna flipped through the pictures. Her grandmother was young and pretty, wearing a cute high ponytail. There were always lots of girls around her. In one picture, her grandmother was holding a flute.

"Oh, you played the flute," Vanna said. Her grandmother had been one of those giggly popular flutes.

"I wanted to play trumpet, but my parents thought I should play the flute."

So maybe there was some brassy toughness in her.

"There's something I know about you that I don't think your parents quite understand." Her grandma's voice didn't have its usual pinch of disappointment. "If you survived summer band, and you hung on through marching season, you've got to be pretty strong."

Vanna was confused, but flattered. "Wasn't Dad in band?"

"Hmph. I suppose. But William went to private school where anyone who wanted to be in band could be. He doesn't know what it's like to be in a big band. Besides, he played oboe."

"I marched tenor sax," Vanna's father said. He was standing in the doorway.

Vanna tensed. She turned another page in the album and tried to ignore her dad.

"Divorce wasn't done in my day, so I don't know how I would have dealt with it," Grandma Reynolds said. "All I can say is be patient. That's what I'm trying to do."

Vanna stared at one of the pictures. "Grandma, you were on the basketball team?"

"Yes, but that's a story for another time." She turned to Vanna's father. "William, I think Vanna wants to go home. Why don't you take her?"

Vanna tried to give back the album.

"No, keep it for a while." Grandma Reynolds gave Vanna a hug and said, "Come and see me again. We can talk about band, and I can tell you how much better it was when I was in it."

Vanna laughed.

"I'm sorry about not visiting. Your mother and I thought you needed time to adjust to the separation. You were pretty angry," Mr. Reynolds explained as he drove Vanna home.

Vanna knew she'd been awful to him. Since they'd

moved to San Antonio she hadn't returned his calls and when they did talk she hardly spoke. And even though he deserved it, she could feel her anger draining.

"I was trying to make things easier, but I don't think it worked. You're not happy here, are you?"

"Not really."

"You can come live with me if you want. I'd love to have you."

Vanna didn't say anything. All she had to do was say yes. No more Spurs. No more Alamo. No more putting up with her mom. No more being poor. Of course, that would also mean no more Olivia, Fatima, and Alex. Instead, Vanna would have Ashlee, Taylor, Caitlyn, and Troy. No more dancing Hamilton band. The Plano bands were rigid military-style marchers.

It was easy to see that in just a short time, she had made better friends in San Antonio than she'd had in Plano. And as much as her mom annoyed her, she couldn't imagine being without her.

Okay, maybe she didn't hate her dad, but she couldn't trust him. What if he married Janet and had a bunch of cute kids? Would he still want Vanna around?

Vanna's father didn't say a word until they pulled up to her apartment complex.

"You don't have to decide anything right now. Just know you have options," he said. "Think about giving me another chance to be in your life."

But Vanna still had questions for her dad. "I don't understand why you cheated on Mom," she blurted out. "If you weren't happy, couldn't you have just told her you wanted a divorce? Did you have to break her heart?"

"I don't know," her father said quietly. "I wasn't thinking. Your mom didn't seem to care what I did. I'd worked with Janet for years. We fell in love. I know it was wrong. I really don't have an excuse. Your mom and I should have gotten a divorce a long time ago, but I didn't want to break up the family and I didn't want to lose you. I knew your mom would take you away."

"All the way to San Antonio?"

"Yes, but at least I have family here. Your granny's been looking out for you. She says you're adjusting well."

"Really?" That meant her grandmother must be calling Vanna's mom to check up on her. She couldn't imagine either of the women enjoying that.

"Your mom says you spend a little too much time watching TV, but you're doing better in school. She worries that you're lonely, with her working a lot."

"Yeah. This place is weird, but I have some good friends."

"Well, then, I'm sure you can use this." He handed her a wrapped box. "Open it."

She ripped open the present. Inside was a silver flip phone.

"Happy birthday. Calls to my phone are free."

"Wow," Vanna said. "Thanks, but an expensive phone isn't—"

"Don't worry," Mr. Reynolds cut her off. "I'm not saying you have to call me. I'll feel better knowing you have it."

Vanna thanked him, got out of the car, and shut the door.

Her father rolled down the window and asked, "Are we going to be okay?"

She looked him directly in the eyes and answered honestly, "I don't know." Then she smiled slightly and added, "Maybe."

He smiled, too. "Well, that sounds good enough to me. I love you, Vanna. You know that, right?"

She turned and dashed up the stairs to her apartment before he could see the tears pricking at her eyes.

"How did it go?" Vanna's mom asked.

"You're home? What happened to Bob?" Vanna had been sure she'd have an hour or two to process everything before her mother came home.

"We just went for coffee. Are you okay?"

"Did you know Dad was going to be there?"

"I'm sorry I didn't warn you. I didn't think I could convince you to go if I'd told you. And if I had gone with you, you probably wouldn't have stayed. It's a little bit harder to run away if you have to wait for the bus to come." Mrs. Reynolds patted the couch next to her. "Come over here and tell me about it."

Vanna sat down. "He gave me a phone. He talked about how much he missed me. He was really nice. But I'm confused and overwhelmed. How am I supposed to forgive him for cheating?"

Her mom sighed. "I don't know. Don't use me as an example. I reacted badly. Since that night, I've been so focused on me and what happened to me that I haven't been taking care of you."

"I can take care of myself," Vanna responded reflexively. Here was her opportunity to let her mom know how she felt. She added, "But it would be nice if you were home more."

"I will be. I'm slowing things down with Bob. I'm not as ready for a relationship as I thought. And I miss us. You and me. The way we used to be."

"Bob okay with that?" Vanna didn't want her mother going through another breakup.

Her mom shrugged. "He'll be fine. About your dad, he loves you." She put an arm around Vanna and squeezed. "But you do whatever makes you feel most comfortable. I'm here for you no matter what."

21

Rosa had a history project due on Friday. A major project worth a huge percentage of her final grade. A project that Rosa wasn't planning on doing. Olivia wouldn't have even known about the project if Rosa hadn't cited it as an example of the stupidity of the public school system. The project was to do a model of one of the local missions.

Olivia had done the same project in seventh grade. She explained that sometimes people have to do things they don't want to, and reminded Rosa that their mother would probably make her drop out of dance if she got a zero on the project and flunked.

Olivia met Rosa at the Alamo on Wednesday after school. Vanna tagged along.

"This is so weird," Vanna said as they approached the shrine. "You would think the Alamo would be out in the middle of nowhere. Not next door to a mall. Ripley's Believe It or Not! is right across the street. It's surreal."

Olivia shrugged. Rosa dug a tape measure out of her backpack.

"I guess," Rosa said. "William Travis was killed right where the post office is now." She pointed at an old-looking building. "And who knows where they burned all the dead bodies. Maybe right where we're standing."

"Ew," Vanna said.

Olivia rolled her eyes and told Vanna, "Ignore her. Why don't you go inside and take a look around since you haven't been here before. We can handle things out here."

Olivia and Rosa busily measured the Alamo. Rosa jerked her head toward a group of tourists reenacting the crossing of Travis's line in the sand. She rolled her eyes.

Olivia shrugged. "Like you never did it." Every public school student in San Antonio went on a field trip to the Alamo in fourth grade. The trips were basically the same. First the class would see *Alamo: The Price of Freedom* (starring Patrick Swazye's brother, Don) at the IMAX. Then they would walk across the street, check out the Alamo, and cross Travis's line. A line he supposedly drew in the dirt when it was clear that reinforcements were not coming and the defenders were facing certain death. The legend says all but one person crossed. A bronzed line lies in front of the main entrance to the shrine. It was impossible to resist. This was a rite of passage for every native San Antonian, like giggling over the naked boy in the Native American diorama at the Witte Museum. At some point, everyone did it.

"We need to measure the distance to that cannon," Rosa announced. Neither girl moved. The cannon looked really far away. "You know, we could wait until Vanna comes back."

"Yeah," Olivia agreed. "So, um, how are things going with you and Virginia? Are you friends again?" As she'd promised Travis, Olivia had spoken to Rosa about patching things up with Virginia. However, she wasn't sure that Rosa had taken her advice.

"We're not friends anymore," Rosa answered with a shrug. No explanation, just a statement.

"You're not even going to try and make up?" Olivia asked. Her concern wasn't simply because Virginia was Travis's sister. As far as Olivia knew, the girls had argued about dance styles. Who throws away a friendship over that?

"Nope. I'm not like you," Rosa said. She didn't look at Olivia. Instead, she concentrated on playing with the tape measure.

"Huh?" What was that supposed to mean?

"I'm not good with friends."

"I'm not either. I only have three," Olivia said. Rosa was the popular one.

"Yeah, but you keep them forever."

"I'm lucky," Olivia explained. It was true that Rosa's

friendships typically lasted only a few months, but if Rosa gave up so easily, she'd never form strong friendships.

Rosa was now looking off in the distance. "Sometimes I wish I could be more like you. Have the same friend since kindergarten or whatever. Someone who knows you that well and still likes you."

"People like you, Rosa."

"Whatever."

Her little sister looked so defeated, Olivia put her arm around her. Rosa accepted the hug with a half-smile. Olivia asked, "Is this really about dance? Did Virginia do something else? Is there a boy involved?" Olivia was pitifully inept when it came to giving advice on boys, but she would do her best.

"No." Rosa sighed. "Virginia just talks way too much and thinks she knows everything. I can't stand her."

Was that all? She was annoying? Everyone's annoying at some point. Olivia chose her words carefully. "You have to be patient with her. She must have some good qualities or you wouldn't have started hanging out with her. Nobody's perfect."

Olivia thought she heard Rosa say, "You are."

"What?" Olivia asked.

"Nothing." Rosa finally looked at Olivia. "Don't worry. I'll make things work with Virginia. You can't lose that connection with Travis."

"Yes, I can." It was Olivia's turn to sigh. "Travis isn't

going to date me just because you're nice to his sister. I need to figure out things with Travis myself. You can't do it for me." That was true. She had to stop sitting around and waiting for Travis to sweep her off her feet.

"I'm your sister. I want you to be happy," Rosa said.

They saw Vanna emerge from the barracks museum and head toward them.

"You know, you're the only person who puts up with me," Rosa said quietly. "I think you're my best friend."

Before Olivia could respond, Vanna joined them and the moment was gone. Vanna was full of questions. Was Travis Martinez named after the Travis from the Alamo? Do people do that often? Were there Bowies and Crocketts running around?

Olivia squeezed her sister's hand and smiled. Deep down Rosa was sweet. But she hardly ever let anyone close enough to see it.

22

Fatima wasn't at the Alamo because right after her flute sectional she had to help her father paint a bathroom pink. This was not her favorite way to spend an evening, but her dad needed her. Her uncle Jorge had double-booked jobs that week. Jorge was already working on a roofing job, which left Fatima's dad alone on the paint job.

Fatima had offered to help, mostly because she enjoyed the alone time with her dad. Plus, her dad's English wasn't very good, so he needed a translator.

They took their dinner outside to get away from the paint fumes. Of course, no matter how much Fatima washed her hands, bits of paint still clung to her skin, which would make her tacos taste a little like paint. She was so hungry she didn't particularly care. Taco, Fatima corrected herself when she opened her paper bag. Her taco would taste painty. Mrs. Garcia had packed Fatima only one skinny bean-and-cheese taco and an apple. An apple. Fatima hated apples. Always had. Her mother knew this.

Fatima momentarily forgot her father was sitting next to her and blurted out in English, "What is wrong with her? An apple? Is she trying to drive me crazy?"

"*Calmate,*" Mr. Garcia said.

Calm down? That was easy for him to say as he unwrapped his *five* tacos, Fatima thought. Her father had two tortillas bulging with *carne guisada*, the brown gravy oozing out, and three fat bean-and-cheese tacos, heavy on the cheese.

"Really, *Papi*, you and I are doing the same work. You are getting paid. I'm not," Fatima ranted. "And she expects me to function on an apple?"

"That is her way," he answered in Spanish even though he seemed to be following Fatima's English well enough.

"Her way of what? Killing me?"

Mr. Garcia gave Fatima an unamused look. "Helping you."

Fatima smiled bitterly. "Oh, yeah, reminding me how fat I am every chance she gets is so helpful. Because how I look is so much more important than how intelligent I am. Why even go to school? Who needs calculus? I'll just starve myself, then get married, have a bunch of kids, and spend my days cleaning houses just like my mom." She filled the last three words with the disgust she was feeling. Alex liked her the way she was, but Fatima's own mother made her feel like a pig.

"*Ya,*" Mr. Garcia said. That one word was all he needed to say to snap Fatima out of her tirade. He hadn't spanked her in years, but the tone he used was enough to remind Fatima that Omar Garcia did not tolerate disrespect.

Fatima sighed. "Sorry," she said. She picked up her taco and took a bite.

"You don't know your mother," Mr. Garcia said. "She is very smart."

"Uh-huh," Fatima mumbled.

"I earn the money, but she makes it last."

Fatima knew her mom took care of the money. Mrs. Garcia paid the bills and budgeted every last penny. Fatima had always thought that just meant her mother was controlling.

"She likes working with numbers. Where do you think you get your brains? Not from me. If she hadn't married me, your mother could have finished school, had a career, and been someone."

"Then why is she so obsessed with how I look? I mean, shouldn't my brain be more important to her?" Fatima pressed.

"Your brain is fine. It doesn't need help."

"Oh, but my body is a disappointment."

Mr. Garcia chewed his food pensively. He looked at Fatima for a while, then said, "It is so difficult here. But with your light skin, if you got skinny, your life would be easier and you would have more opportunities." He looked down at his dark hands.

When he looked back up, there was pain in his eyes. Fatima felt a lump form in her throat. Her parents really believed they were helping her. They thought being skinny would make her look less Mexican? "*Papi*, it's not like that anymore," Fatima tried to explain. "It's not the sixties. Skin color isn't that important here. Just about everyone in San Antonio is part Mexican."

"*Ay*, Fatima," he said, "it is still important. But you don't need to worry." He smiled, but there was still sadness in his eyes. "Be patient with your mother. She gave her dreams to you."

Fatima didn't know how to respond to that. She picked up the apple she had scorned earlier. That apple was her mother's way of providing a better life for Fatima. Other parents may pressure their kids into going to Ivy League schools or becoming star athletes. Fatima's mother pressured her to eat apples.

"I will," Fatima told her father. She took a bite of the apple.

"Here, have a taco." Mr. Garcia gave Fatima one of his *carne guisada* tacos. "I don't need to eat that much either." He patted his round belly.

On the way home that night, Fatima made her father pick up a copy of the *San Antonio Express-News*. They didn't usually buy the newspaper since neither of her parents was comfortable reading English.

At home, Fatima found Juan and Diego asleep and Luli watching TV. Mrs. Garcia was cleaning the kitchen. Her dad immediately headed for the shower. Fatima sat down at the kitchen table and pulled out the S.A. Life section of the newspaper. Mrs. Garcia was not too happy to have a paint-splattered, sweat-soaked Fatima sitting at the clean kitchen table.

Instead of reacting to her mother's complaining, Fatima asked, "*Mami*, have you ever played Sudoku?"

"Su-*que*?" her mother responded irritably. "I don't know *japonese*."

"You don't have to speak Japanese," Fatima said. "It's a number game."

"Games? Do I look like I have time for games?"

"Just try it. I'll finish up the kitchen. I think you'll like Sudoku."

Her mother sank into the chair next to Fatima, looking skeptical. Be patient, Fatima reminded herself. It was probably the first time Mrs. Garcia had sat down all day.

Fatima explained the basics of Sudoku. Her mother caught on quickly. She took the pencil and newspaper away from Fatima and began filling in the puzzle on her own. Fatima watched the tiredness gradually leave her mother's face. She quietly stepped away from the table and finished up the dishes. Mrs. Garcia's brow furrowed in concentration and she grumbled a bit, but there was a spark in her eyes that Fatima had never realized was missing.

23

Toe, heel, heel, toe, heel, stomp. Toe, heel, heel, toe, heel, stomp. Olivia repeated the step to herself as her dance teacher sped up the rhythm, but her feet weren't cooperating. During her two-year vacation from dance classes, she seemed to have lost all her coordination. It didn't help that Javier, her dance teacher, didn't speak much English. Olivia had started taking classes with him when she was five years old. You would think in all that time he would have picked up more English. His favorite English word seemed to be *again*. He said it about a million times during class.

"*Pecho al techo,*" Javier said and poked Olivia between the shoulder blades. Chest to the roof. Olivia had to remember her posture. There were so many things to remember, and they hadn't even added arms to the step, much less castanets.

Olivia thought of Vanna and how bored she must be.

Vanna had come along to class because Mrs. Reynolds wanted her to get involved in more activities. One wall of the studio was covered in mirrors. The opposite wall had huge windows that looked into a waiting room where parents could watch the classes. Every once in a while Olivia would glance back at the windows to check on Vanna. Poor Vanna was in the waiting room doing homework. At least Rosa was keeping her company. Rosa's more advanced class didn't start until after Olivia's class.

"What on earth is he doing to her?" Vanna asked Rosa. Olivia's chubby dance teacher was holding Olivia's bangs while she did a turn.

"Teaching her to do a *quebrada* turn," Rosa said. "Olivia needs to bend her back more and keep her head still."

"But doesn't it hurt?" Vanna couldn't help wincing as she watched Olivia try to pull her head up when she turned. The dance teacher pulled her head down.

"Not really, unless you fall," Rosa said. She didn't bother looking up from her work again.

No one seemed very concerned that the teacher was literally pulling Olivia's hair out. Olivia's mother was grading papers and chatting with the other mothers. The other dancers in the class were lining up ready to get their hair pulled, too.

"It's the best way to learn them," Rosa added. "They look really cool when you do them right."

Vanna decided dance class was not her thing.

"The first half of class is always technique," Olivia said when she came over to chat during a break. "It's really boring."

"Got to learn your scales before you can play a symphony," Rosa mumbled.

Olivia rolled her eyes. "Anyway, we're going to do choreography with music now."

The second half of the class was much more interesting. The class was doing a *malagueña*. Olivia twirled across the floor while keeping in formation and in step with the other dancers. It was like marching band, but in skirts. Olivia wriggled her hips and moved like Vanna had never seen before.

When the teacher yelled, *"Esmile!"* Olivia plastered a flirtatious smile on her face. She danced with such confidence that Vanna hardly recognized her. Olivia certainly didn't look like a girl too shy to talk to a boy.

"I had no idea she could do that," Vanna said.

"Half of dancing is acting. Olivia's good at pretending to be whatever people want her to be," Rosa replied.

If only Travis could see this side of Olivia. He wouldn't stand a chance.

24

The homecoming game had been on Friday night. It had been close. They had played their rival, Thomas Jefferson High School, and won, barely. Now the big excitement was that evening's dance. Everyone in band was looking forward to it. Everyone except Olivia.

She wasn't going. She'd asked her mom and the answer was no. The dance happened to be at the exact time as Rosa's first performance at the Arneson River Theatre. As busy as Mrs. Silverstein had been lately, she was big on family. There was no way she'd let Olivia out of going to see Rosa dance, especially since Rosa went to every one of Olivia's football games. But Olivia had to go to the dance. Travis had practically said he would be looking for her. Maybe if she asked again her mother would realize how important the dance was. Maybe, but Olivia wasn't holding her breath.

Olivia forced herself to concentrate on her current task. She sprayed Rosa's slicked-back hair with a ton of hair spray and began working on her bun.

"Make sure you're ready by six," their mother said. "Gloria will be here to pick you up then. Help Rosa load the costumes and everything." Their mother had phoned during her break at the jewelry store. Olivia had her on speakerphone so they could both hear her while she worked on Rosa's hair. "I should be off work in time to see your group, Rosa," their mother continued. "Olivia, I might be late, so make sure you save me a seat near the aisle."

"Um, about tonight, Mom," Olivia said, rolling a section of Rosa's hair and pinning it into place. "I really want to go to the dance at school. Vanna's mom would take me and bring me home."

"We've already had this discussion. My answer hasn't changed," Mrs. Silverstein responded.

"Ow!" Rosa yelped when Olivia jammed a bobby pin into Rosa's hair a little too roughly.

"Sorry, I just wanna make sure it stays," Olivia mumbled.

"You can't miss your sister's show. She's worked too hard," their mother said.

Olivia wrapped a thick hairnet around Rosa's bun. "But—"

"There will be other dances," her mother interrupted.

"Okay," Olivia said. Why had she even bothered asking again?

"I have to run. My break's almost over. Make sure Rosa is ready on time. Love you both. Bye." Mrs. Silverstein hung up.

"I need a red flower in my hair for the first dance." Rosa paused, then added, "It's all right with me if you skip the show. I'll tell Mom you got sick with a stomach thing. She won't expect you to go. The show's over at ten, but you know how long it takes me to get all my junk together, so we probably won't be back until around ten-thirty. You could go to the dance and be home before Mom even noticed."

Rosa made it sound so easy. Just go. No one will ever know. But Olivia didn't do that sort of thing. She hardly ever broke the rules. She didn't ditch her responsibilities. Her mother told her to be there, so she would go to the show. Olivia always did what she was told. Always.

She sighed and picked out a gigantic artificial red rose from Rosa's box of headpieces. The rose would make Rosa look even more beautiful. With flawless creamy skin, huge lips, and heavy eyeliner accenting her dark brown eyes, she looked like the perfect Spanish dancer. Olivia could never hope to look like that.

As she was pinning the rose into her sister's hair, Fatima and Vanna called.

"It's no big deal. I would probably just sit around all night anyway," Olivia told them. She held the phone in the crook of her neck as she finished up Rosa's hair.

"My mom and I are picking you up," Fatima said. "Then we'll get ready at Vanna's."

"But I have to go to Rosa's show," Olivia said, patting Rosa on the head, signaling she was finished. "You guys have fun. You can tell me about it tomorrow."

"Olivia, sometimes I think you're brain-dead or something," Rosa said as she left the room. "Just remember, Mom and I will be home at ten-thirty."

"Wait, Olivia, did I hear your sister say what I think she did? Now you have no excuse!" Leave it to Vanna to pick up on everything.

"Perfect, I'll come and get you as soon as my mom finishes my dress. She's hemming it or something," Fatima said.

"I don't have anything to wear," Olivia said lamely.

"Don't worry. We'll take care of everything at my house. Fatima, just get her over here," Vanna said.

25

"*Mira,*" Fatima's mother said, turning Fatima toward the full-length mirror, "look at how pretty you are." They were putting the finishing touches on Fatima's dress before the dance. Her mother had let Fatima pick out the pattern and the fabric, and then spent the last month sewing it.

"Amazing. How did you do it?" Fatima asked. "I don't really look *that* fat." It was a simple knee-length black dress with a small slit on the right leg. Her mother had tailored it so it flattered the curves Fatima usually hid under baggy T-shirts. Fatima's flabby stomach was still flabby, but the dress camouflaged it.

"*Callate,*" her mother said, lightly swatting Fatima's arms. "When you stand up straight and smile, you are beautiful. You have been smiling a lot more lately and you stopped hunching *como una vieja*. I noticed. *Hija*, so maybe you're not a stick like Olivia. You're a woman."

The last time her mother had told Fatima that she was beautiful was the day of Fatima's first communion. In first grade!

"Um, *Mamita*, you're not dying or anything, are you?" Fatima asked.

"What? No! I have to be dying to say something nice?" Fatima smirked.

"Okay," her mother said, "I'm a little tough on you, but that's because I want you to work hard. You have so much going for you, I don't want you to waste it."

Fatima, now confused, said, "And by being fat I'm wasting my life?"

"No," her mother replied. She sat down on the bed and sighed. "Your weight is the only thing I can help you with. I can't help you with school. I don't know enough English. I can't give you money for nice clothes or things. I can't read music, so I can't help you with your flute. All I can do is cook, clean, and have babies. *Y parece* all I taught Lupe was to have babies."

"Don't you miss her?" Fatima asked quietly. "Don't you worry?"

"Of course I do. *Pero* she made her choice."

"The baby's really cute," Fatima said. "You should meet her. You'd fall in love."

"I have."

"You met Chula? When? How?" Fatima was shocked.

"Do you think I could live knowing I had a grandbaby and not visit her? I do many things while you are at school

162

that you do not know about. Ninfa takes care of the baby while Lupe is working. I go and help."

"Does Lupe know?"

"No, she wants to punish me, so I let her think she is."

Her mother had a secret daytime life. Fatima had thought Mrs. Garcia just cleaned all day.

"Does Dad visit, too?"

"No, he is not ready. *Es tan orguioso.*"

He's too proud? That was her mother's excuse. "What's the big deal? You were about the same age as Lupe when you had her," Fatima said.

"But we were married. To your father, what happened with Lupe was his fault. He did not take care of his family. He won't forgive her until he forgives himself."

"In the meantime, what about Lupe and Chula?"

"*Ay,* that name!" Mrs. Garcia cringed. "So many beautiful names and she picks that." She shook her head. "Ninfa says Lupe is a good mother. And why wouldn't she be? Lupe had plenty of practice. She took care of you, Luli, and the twins. She can call if she needs me."

"You should call her first. You shouldn't be so tough on her."

"I am tough on all my children. I have to be. My *mamá* left school to work after third grade. Your father made it to the sixth grade. I wasn't much better. But, Fatima, you are smart. You can go to college. You have so many advantages here. I want more for you. I want you to be happy."

"You're not happy?"

"Of course I am," her mother said. She patted Fatima's hand, then stood up. "But it was difficult."

"I'm happy. Maybe not all the time, but I know I'm lucky. I—" Fatima was cut off by a screaming Luli.

"*Mami!*" Luli shrieked. "The boys are playing with dog *caca* again! They are writing with it on the sidewalk!"

"*Dios mio!* At least they're not eating it. Fatima, *andale*. Hurry up and finish getting ready. We have to pick up Olivia," her mother said, rushing out.

"I am ready," Fatima said to the empty room.

26

"Tonight's the night. Finally, Travis is going to realize his love for you," Vanna announced as she dragged Olivia and Fatima into her bedroom.

"Yeah, right," Olivia said.

"Seriously, Vanna, you're putting a lot of pressure on one night," Fatima said.

"I saw the way he looked at Olivia the other day. He was interested in more than discussing your sisters." Vanna laughed as she danced over to her closet.

"I wish I'd been there," Fatima said.

"It was so cute. He dragged out all this stuff about their sisters, just so he could talk to her," Vanna said.

"The guy was passing time until he found his friends." Olivia was still feeling guilty about disobeying her mother. She had finally done something wild and she couldn't even enjoy it.

"Olivia," Vanna said, "what's with the negativity?"

"I don't know. I guess I don't want to get my hopes up." Olivia didn't think she could handle Travis rejecting her after all these years of liking him.

"If you give him one of your dance class smiles, he'll melt," Vanna teased.

"That's just for the stage. It's not really me," Olivia said.

"I think it might be," Fatima said. Olivia wasn't all that shy when Travis wasn't around.

Vanna surveyed the contents of her closet. "I don't think any of my clothes will fit you. Have a seat." Olivia obediently flopped down on Vanna's bed, and Fatima joined her.

"Mom! I need your help in here! And bring some safety pins!" Vanna shouted.

"Coming!" her mother called.

"She's getting ready for a date," Vanna told Fatima and Olivia. "Bob's gonna pick us up. They're going out to dinner while we're at the dance. Ever since I saw my dad, she's been trying to get more involved in my life. She's asking about my grades and talking to my teachers."

"That's good, right?" Olivia said.

"It's weird. She's even decided to join band boosters and wear the dorky shirt and everything." Vanna rolled her eyes. "I'll believe it when I see it. Anyway, tonight she's working her schedule around us. She'll pick us up from the dance at ten. That should give us plenty of time to get Olivia home before her mom, and we'll only miss an hour of the dance."

"Thanks," Olivia said. "I'm sorry you guys have to leave early. I hate messing things up for y'all."

"It's not a big deal. If you stay until the end of the dance, you have to help clean up. So we probably would have left early anyway," Fatima said.

"You won't mind cutting short your big night out with Alex?" Olivia asked.

"Not really. I'm not even sure it's a real date," Fatima replied, irritated with herself for feeling insecure.

"Well, you look incredible. I'm sure he'll be drooling," Vanna said.

Fatima blushed and mumbled, "Thanks to control-top panty hose."

"But you could use a little eye makeup," Vanna said.

Vanna's mother glided into the room. She, like Vanna, already had her makeup on, but was still wearing a bathrobe.

"What have we got to work with?" she asked.

"I don't have anything that will fit Olivia, Mom, but we have to make her look gorgeous. Remember Travis, the guy who's in love with her but doesn't realize it yet? We need to draw him to her so she can work her magic." Vanna pulled Fatima's glasses off.

"What magic?" Olivia interrupted.

"All my stuff's a size six," Vanna said, ignoring Olivia's question as she applied eyeliner on Fatima. "It'll just hang on her. You're what, a size two, Olivia?"

"Yeah, but I don't have any magic."

"Of course you do. Now, what should we do about wardrobe?" Vanna said. She scrutinized Fatima's eyes.

"Don't look at me. She'd be swimming in my clothes," Fatima said. "Can I have my glasses back yet? I need to see the damage."

"All right, girls, come with me," Mrs. Reynolds said. "Let's see if I have anything. I was a two before I had Vanna, and I hate to throw clothes out." She led them to her bedroom. "Please excuse the mess. I couldn't decide what to wear." There were skirts, blouses, and dresses everywhere.

"Let me see . . ." Vanna's mother said, flipping through the clothes hanging in her closet. "Ah. Perfect." She pulled out a short spaghetti-strap red dress and held it against her body. "I wore this ages ago, before I got married. Danced all night with a Bolivian who looked like George Clooney. I haven't felt that good in a long time. I suppose that's why I never parted with it." She handed the dress to Olivia.

"Thanks," Olivia said. "I'll have it back to you by to-morrow."

"Keep it. There's no way it would fit over my hips now. You might as well get some use out of it. Bob will be here soon, so let's finish getting you ready."

The time flew by. Vanna managed to force some eye shadow on Fatima. Then she worked on Olivia's makeup, while her mother tackled Olivia's hair and Fatima painted Olivia's fingernails "Flamenco Red." Olivia felt like a movie star. Sure, Vanna almost glued Olivia's eyes shut while applying false eyelashes, and Mrs. Reynolds spent most of the time trying to convince Olivia to cut her hair, but Olivia had never felt so pampered.

The dress fit perfectly, clinging in all the right places. When she finally looked at herself, she didn't recognize the long-legged creature in the mirror. She looked almost as pretty as Rosa.

It's just a dress, Olivia told herself. Tonight she would go home, take it off, and go back to normal. Still, looking in that mirror, she didn't feel like pathetic, fatherless Olivia. For a little while at least, she was Olivia, the gorgeous siren.

27

Bob, who introduced himself as Roberto Hernandez, drove them to the dance in his silver BMW. Olivia had never seen a BMW up close, much less been inside one. When they pulled up in front of the school, heads turned to see who was arriving in such a nice car. She hadn't even set foot in the cafeteria and she was already having the best time of her life.

Alex was waiting for them in the hallway outside the cafeteria. "It took y'all long enough. I was beginning to think . . ." He stopped talking when Fatima stepped out from behind Olivia and Vanna. She'd been hiding and was now self-consciously tugging on her skirt, sure everyone would take one look at her and laugh. Her earlier confidence had evaporated as soon as she had stepped out of Bob's car.

Alex stared silently at her, and Fatima stared at him. He

looked good—really good. He wasn't wearing his glasses and she could see how green his eyes were. Alex was looking at her like she was beautiful. And for once in her life Fatima felt beautiful.

Fatima wanted to tell him how great he looked, but all that came out of her was a soft "Hey."

Alex smiled and said, "Hey."

Someone cleared her throat and Fatima realized Olivia and Vanna were standing there grinning while she and Alex gawked at each other.

Alex recovered first. "Let's go in," he said. He held out his hand and Fatima took it. He led her into the cafeteria and over to a table as far away from the DJ's blaring speakers as possible. Fatima and Alex sat on one side of the table, Olivia and Vanna on the other.

"You look great, Alex," Olivia said.

"Thanks. Y'all clean up pretty nice, too." He looked at Fatima. "You look amazing."

Alex had his arm across the back of Fatima's chair. He was close to her. Very close. She could smell his cologne. Fatima wished she had thought to put on perfume.

"We need to wait for a good song," Vanna was saying.

"What counts as a good song?" Alex asked. "Nothing too girlie, I hope."

"We'll know it when we hear it," Vanna replied. She looked around for Travis. Vanna wanted both of her friends to have a perfect night, and it seemed obvious that everything was going well for Fatima.

Olivia squealed when the peppy opening of Selena's "Bidi Bidi Bom Bom" rang out. "This is such a Travis song. We have to dance."

Vanna had played this song every week in the halftime show, but never really paid attention to the words. The lyrics were all in Spanish. Even though Vanna couldn't understand it, she knew that if Olivia called it a "Travis song," it must be about unrequited love. Olivia had made Vanna listen to many Travis songs.

"Come on. It's from the halftime show," Olivia added.

That wasn't much of an enticement for Vanna. Selena was fine on the field, but on the dance floor?

"I don't know how to dance to this kind of music," Vanna protested.

"This is a cumbia. It's so easy. You don't have to dance with a partner. We could all do it together," Olivia said.

A cumbia, Vanna found out, involved groups of people linking hands and doing a step-ball-change-type move while circling the dance floor. It was not quite as easy in heels as Olivia made it seem. Not surprisingly, a few bars into the song, Fatima and Alex broke off from the group to do their own thing.

Fatima was not the best dancer, but she could do a mean cumbia. Her father loved Tejano music and would take any opportunity to dance with one of his *chicas*. Fatima had been cumbia-ing almost as long as she'd been walking. Apparently, so had Alex, which wasn't surprising since Tejano music was a staple at just about every San Antonio wedding, *quinceañera*, birthday party, and picnic. The fact that Vanna didn't know how to dance to it was a sign that she hadn't been to enough parties.

The blissful beat and rapid turns made Fatima giddy. By the end of the song, Fatima's heart was going *bidi bidi bom bom*.

"I just spotted him," Vanna shouted over the music as she steadied Olivia. Olivia had tried to twist too low during "The Twist" and had almost fallen over.

"Really? Where?" Olivia asked, automatically knowing that "him" meant Travis.

"Two o'clock."

"Where?" Olivia had absolutely no idea where two o'clock was.

"Over to the right, by the stairs."

Olivia spotted him standing with Cecelia. She sighed loudly and hopelessly.

"Okay, here's the plan. We are going to dance over and you're going to make eye contact with him."

"But I'm terrible at that."

"Not tonight. This is your night, remember? Everything you do is going to work out. Don't worry about impressing him. Act natural, and fate will take care of the rest," Vanna said.

"Okay. Let's do it," Olivia said, and Vanna directed them to the perfect spot.

They danced for a few minutes before Olivia had enough courage to glance over at Travis. He was watching her as he talked with Cecelia. Olivia felt a thrill race through her. She smiled at him, then looked away. This is heaven, she thought. She'd made eye contact with him and hadn't blushed or tripped or done anything embarrassing.

After about ten more minutes of dancing, Vanna suggested they get a drink.

"Well?" Fatima asked.

"I did it!" Olivia felt great.

"You haven't even talked to him yet," Alex said. He handed Fatima a cup of punch.

"It doesn't matter. In fact, it's better this way. I don't think I could actually come up with anything to say to him."

"Well, you better think of something quick because he's coming this way," Alex said, looking over Olivia's shoulder.

"Hey, Menchaca," Travis said to Alex as he approached the table, "how does a guy like you score three dates?"

"Not by wearing a tie like yours." Alex put his arm around Fatima's waist, bold as could be. A most boyfriend-like move, in Fatima's eyes.

"Hey"—Travis looked down at his striped tie—"my little sister swore this tie was cool. It's a knockoff of some Italian designer."

"Little sisters don't know much about attracting the ladies," Alex said.

Fatima rolled her eyes.

Travis laughed. "And how are you ladies tonight?" he asked, ladling himself a cup of punch.

"Good," Fatima said, and beamed at Alex.

Olivia's mind went blank, so she just nodded slightly. Vanna shot her a look that screamed, "Talk to him!" But Olivia didn't.

"This punch is nasty," Travis said and put his cup back on the table.

He was getting ready to walk away, Olivia could tell. He was going to leave and never talk to her again because she was boring. She had to think of something to say. Anything.

"How do you like working in a movie theater?" she blurted out. It was a lame question, but at least he would have to answer her.

"It's a way to make money." Travis shrugged. "I'm trying to fix up my car, and it's costing me a fortune."

"Is it hard work?"

"Not usually. You know the Bijou shows mostly arty movies. The people who go see them tend to be older and fairly neat. But once in a while we get an annoying kid movie. Little kids like to throw massive amounts of popcorn and candy on the floor when they watch a movie. I hate cleaning up after those."

"I like the occasional kid movie," Olivia said. "They're not all annoying."

"As far as I can tell, you like pretty much any movie. I can't figure out your taste."

"It's really not that complicated. My family takes turns picking movies," Olivia explained. "I pick kid movies or happy romances. Rosa goes for anything weird or tragic. And my mom likes lots of violence."

Olivia and Travis talked for a while about movies. Travis was in the middle of criticizing the latest zombie movie when Olivia heard the strumming of a guitar as it played the opening chords of a hauntingly romantic song.

"I can't believe they're playing this song," she said, not even registering that she was interrupting Travis.

Alex winked at Fatima.

Fatima explained to a puzzled Travis, "She loves this song."

"What is it?" Travis asked.

"Only one of the greatest songs ever recorded," Olivia said. " 'Sleepwalk' by Santo and Johnny. You'll recognize it in a minute."

"This is a cool song. Let's dance," Alex said. He led Fatima away. Other kids started pairing off and slow dancing.

Olivia took a deep breath. "I have to dance to this," she said, then asked casually, "How about it, Travis?"

Time halted as she awaited his answer. She ceased to breathe. All sound faded. Everything stopped. Everything except Olivia's heart, which beat in triple time.

"Sure."

As Travis took Olivia's hand and led her to the dance floor, she smiled at Vanna and challenged her, "Don't you have someone to talk to?"

Vanna grinned. "I guess I do."

Vanna watched the couples dance for a while. She decided not to feel sorry for herself. If Olivia could find the courage to dance with Travis, and Fatima could dump the hottest guy in school, then Vanna could certainly get off her butt and start putting that whole Troy mess behind her. She had promised Olivia she'd talk to Jake. No time like the present.

Vanna was surprised Jake had come to something as cheesy as a school dance. He seemed too hip for that kind of thing, but there he was, standing alone in a vintage army jacket, faded jeans, and an Air T-shirt.

Vanna approached him with a cool "Hey."

He gave her a "Hey" back, but that was it.

"Where'd you get your shirt?" Vanna asked. That sounded like a perfectly legitimate reason to seek out someone. Where did he get all his cool stuff?

"Austin," Jake answered. "My sister goes to UT, so I'm up there a lot."

"Oh, I thought maybe there was a place in town."

"Are you into them?" Jake pointed at his shirt.

Truthfully, Vanna was more of a pop girl and had no idea what Air was, but she could broaden her horizons. "A little."

"It's hard to describe their sound. I would say trip hop electronica with indie rock mixed in. You think?"

Vanna nodded. She had no idea what he had just said, but it sounded cool.

"I thought all you North Texans just listened to country," Jake said.

"A common misconception." Troy had been really into country music.

"You should check out Kasabian. They're like Air crossed with Led Zeppelin."

"Thanks, I will." Vanna had heard of Led Zeppelin, at least.

"Have you ever been to First Friday?" he asked.

"No. What is it?"

"It's this thing they have over in Southtown on the first Friday of every month. There's free art shows, local bands, and all sorts of stuff for sale. Very Austiny feel. You'd probably like it. I'll let you know next time my friends and I go."

"Cool," Vanna said. Very, very cool.

Olivia's only prior experience with slow dancing involved sitting at every single dance of her entire life and pathetically watching other people slow dance. She found out it was really hard to be cool when Travis's hands were on her hips. Her hands were on his broad shoulders. She wanted to remember every sensation.

"Your hair looks pretty like that," Travis said.

"Vanna's mom did it for me," Olivia said, grateful that he had broken the silence.

"Great outfit."

"Vanna and her mom put it together."

Travis smiled at her. "Olivia, take a compliment. Just say thanks."

"Thanks." She knew she was blushing. "You look nice, too."

"Thank you."

Silence.

This is not going well, Olivia thought.

Travis leaned close to her, and whispered, "Check out Alex and Fatima."

It took Olivia a moment to register what he said because having his lips so near caused goose bumps to pop up all over her. When she did look at Fatima and Alex, she saw they were dancing with no space between their bodies.

"Hmmm. Interesting," Olivia said.

"Yeah," Travis said. "I never thought those two would get together."

Olivia felt a pressure on her right foot that painfully smashed her toes. She involuntarily yelped and hopped back, but still managed to keep her hands on his shoulders.

"Did I just step on your foot?" Travis winced. "I'm sorry."

"That's okay. My feet are tough," Olivia said. Poor guy really couldn't dance.

"Next time you and your friends go to the movies, you should let me know. I could get you some passes," Travis offered.

"Thanks." Now Olivia had a reason to seek him out again.

"So, you really like this song?"

"Yeah," she replied. Talking must make him feel more comfortable, she thought, because he sure was talking a lot.

"I didn't know anyone still liked this type of music."

"Yeah, I guess I'm a little behind the times," Olivia said, then laughed.

"The only time I've ever heard this song was in that movie, you know, *La Bamba.* My mom loves that movie," Travis told her.

"So does mine."

"They play this song at the end when everyone finds out Ritchie Valens is dead."

"Yeah. Right at the end of the song his brother runs to that bridge and yells—"

"Ritchie!" they said at the same time, and laughed.

"I know," Olivia said. "It reminds everyone of that scene, and it was the saddest part of the movie. But it makes me think of how cool life was in the fifties and sixties. You know, the way people dressed and danced."

"Yeah, I guess so. I'm not very good at fifties dancing. Here, let me try." He twirled her around. Then he put his hand on her waist and held her other hand. "This is more old-school."

As the last mournful notes of the song sounded, Travis clumsily dipped Olivia.

"You're pretty good," she whispered.

"Yeah, right, but thanks."

He was still holding her when the next song, an enthusiastic Tejano polka, began. They stared at each other for a few seconds, ignoring the couples circling around them.

Vanna suddenly appeared and grabbed Olivia's right arm. "Olivia, it's after ten."

"What? It can't be," Olivia said. She should have already left. How could time have passed so quickly?

"What's wrong?" Travis asked. Olivia couldn't help but notice he was still holding her left hand.

"I have to leave," she explained.

"Your curfew's ten o'clock?"

"It's a long story," Olivia answered. She felt his grip loosen and his hand drop away from hers. She wanted to grab it and keep dancing with him. Wanted to stay in that red dress in the too warm cafeteria, and not be shy, ordinary Olivia.

"Her mom's real strict," Vanna told Travis.

"Too bad," Travis said.

"So, thanks for the dance. I, um, had a great time." Olivia avoided looking Travis in the eyes.

"Me, too. I hope you don't get in trouble," he said. He looked slightly confused as he walked away.

That wasn't what Travis was supposed to do. He was supposed to kiss her goodbye or at least walk her to the car, not stroll away with his hands in his pockets.

"Sorry, honey," Vanna said, "but we have to go. This isn't bad. You'll leave him wanting more."

"I guess."

Vanna led Olivia off the dance floor. "I talked to Jake tonight, and let's just say there may be a date in my future."

"Really?" Olivia noticed that Vanna looked excited. "Yay, Vanna. When?"

"I'll tell you all about it in the car. Looks like it was a good night for everyone," Vanna said as they found Fatima and Alex in the hallway. It was clearly not a good time to interrupt.

"We'll meet you outside in a few minutes," Olivia said. She and Vanna rushed out.

"We have to get Olivia home," Fatima told Alex. Fatima hadn't thought it would be so hard to leave early. She liked being in Alex's arms.

"I know," he said, but didn't move.

"I really have to go," Fatima said, and started to step away.

"Hold on." Alex stopped her. Then he leaned down and kissed her.

28

When Olivia walked into the house, her mom was asleep on the living room couch and Rosa was watching TV. Olivia wasn't looking forward to seeing her mom's disappointment or to the grounding she would surely get as punishment, but she felt free. She wasn't perfect anymore.

"I tried to stall her as much as possible, but we were done early," Rosa said, giving Olivia a sympathetic look. "I promised to wake her up as soon as you came home, but I want to hear about the dance first. How was it?"

"Incredible," Olivia answered.

"You danced with him?"

"Yeah." Olivia smiled.

"Thank the Lord! So, are you two going to go out?"

Perfect Olivia might have felt like she had disappointed everyone by not making Travis fall madly in love with her after just one dance. Of course, Perfect Olivia wouldn't have even danced with him because she was too afraid of failing. Human Olivia was quite pleased with how things had turned out. She told Rosa as much, saying, "We're working on it. He doesn't really know me that well, yet."

"Yet?"

Olivia only broadened her smile.

Rosa made a noise—a sort of cross between a squeal and a giggle. "You rock!" She squeezed Olivia's hand.

Mrs. Silverstein snored loudly, drawing the girls' attention.

Olivia's smile faded. "We better get this over with."

"I'll wake her, but don't worry. I got your back." Rosa shook their mother awake. "Mom, she's home. And she's fine."

"Do you have any idea how I felt when I got home and you weren't here? Rosa said you were sick," their mother demanded, going from sleeping to scolding instantly.

"She freaked out for about five minutes," Rosa said, "then she fell asleep."

"I went to the dance," Olivia said.

"Why would you disobey me like that? And lie to me? You're not that type of girl." Mrs. Silverstein shook her head.

"It was my idea," Rosa interjected. "You weren't being fair, Mom. And really, what's the big deal? It's not like this is the only time I'll ever dance at the Arneson. I plan on having a very long career."

Olivia smiled gratefully at Rosa, but she wouldn't let her take the blame.

"I really wanted to be in both places—the dance and Rosa's show," Olivia explained. "Rosa didn't mind me missing one show. She understood how important this was. You said there would be other dances, but not until next year."

"I don't understand. You didn't make it sound this important."

"It was," Olivia said.

Mrs. Silverstein let out an exasperated sigh. "Then why didn't you fight me more?"

"I don't know. I didn't want you to be mad at me."

"Since when do you worry about making me mad?"

Olivia didn't answer. How could she explain how much she worried about making her mom's life easier without making her mom feel bad? How could she explain how angry she was at being expected to do everything and how guilty she felt for being angry? How could she explain how hurt she was that her mom took her for granted? So Olivia didn't say anything, but Rosa did.

"Since Dad died," Rosa said.

"What?" Mrs. Silverstein asked.

"Think about it, Mom. When was the last time you got mad at Olivia?"

"I don't know. It's been a long time." She turned to Olivia. "Do you remember?"

Of course Olivia remembered. She was shocked that Rosa remembered. Olivia hadn't thought Rosa had been paying attention that day. Rosa had been watching *Gone with the Wind* in her bedroom.

Rosa whispered, "You want me to tell her?"

"No," Olivia said. This was something Olivia needed to handle herself. "It was the day after Dad died. You wanted me to stay home to help you pick out a casket and buy black clothes, but I went to school instead." She had gone to escape all the sadness and to pretend everything was normal.

"Oh, right. But Olivia, I wasn't really thinking then. I was too upset. Whatever I said . . ." Mrs. Silverstein trailed off as if trying to remember.

Olivia remembered every word. "You said that I was too selfish to help, and that you needed someone you could depend on. You told me that if I didn't grow up and start pulling my weight, you'd fall apart and I wouldn't have any parents left."

Neither her mom nor Rosa said a word.

Olivia looked at her mom and tried to explain. "I tried. Really, I've tried to make things easier. Even tonight, I thought if you didn't find out you wouldn't be worried or disappointed. I'm sorry." Olivia was suddenly exhausted. She wanted to go to bed and never talk about this again.

"Olivia—" Mrs. Silverstein began.

"I'm really tired. Could we please talk about punishment tomorrow?" Olivia interrupted.

"Sure. We'll talk about everything tomorrow."

29

Sunday afternoon, Vanna's mother took her on an outing. They pulled up in front of a small house with a weed-infested yard. The paint was peeling and the windows were boarded up. There was graffiti sprayed along the walls.

"Is this where you used to live?" Vanna asked.

"Yeah, when we finally settled," Mrs. Reynolds said. "We moved around a lot when I was little. At one time, I think we even lived in a trailer."

"How come you wanted to show me this?"

"You've got your grandma giving you photo albums telling you all about that side of the family. I thought you might want to see where I came from, what my life was like before I met your dad. Sadly, this is it. You see why I was dying to get away."

"Did it look like this back then?"

"The windows weren't boarded up, and there wasn't

graffiti, but, yeah, pretty much. My mama used to have her beauty shop here." She pointed to a room that jutted out from the side of the house.

"Cool," Vanna said, because her mom seemed to want her to say something. Vanna couldn't picture Claire Reynolds ever living in a place like this. Sure, their apartment was cheap, but it wasn't depressing.

"I hated it," her mom continued. "The house would smell like that chemical she used to perm hair. I tried to spend the least amount of time at home as possible. Then I went off to college, but it was close enough that she could still take care of me."

The situation sounded kind of sad to Vanna, but her mom didn't seem sad. She was describing her childhood as casually as someone would discuss the weather.

"After she died, I didn't have anyone to take care of me anymore. That's when your father stepped in. We'd been dating for a while and he rescued me. He handled all the funeral arrangements and bills. Then he up and married me, and I had no more worries. I was dependent on him for everything. I grew to hate it and so did he."

"Well, you're not dependent on him anymore," Vanna said with satisfaction.

"But I am. I'm barely making above minimum wage at the bank. And I'm letting your dad take care of the bills when I can't make ends meet."

"Dad is supposed to pay child support," Vanna pointed out.

"I know, but he doesn't have to pay my rent. Dahlia's divorced. She's independent. Why aren't I?"

"You shouldn't be so hard on yourself, Mom."

"I've decided to go back to school. A couple of night classes or something."

"What are you going to study?"

"Business."

"Really?" Vanna asked. Her mother didn't seem the type to be interested in business.

"That's what I was majoring in before I dropped out. I'm good at it. I enjoy it."

"What are you going to do when you finish?"

Mrs. Reynolds shrugged. "Get a better job, first off. Then my dream of dreams is to open my own business. A bar or restaurant or—"

"A beauty shop?" Vanna offered.

"I wish you could have met your grandmother. You would have liked her. She was very independent."

Vanna nodded.

Mrs. Reynolds put her arm around Vanna. "Take one last look at where you came from. I heard they're demolishing this whole block to make room for some hotel. Although I don't know who would want to stay on this side of town."

As they drove away, Vanna watched her mother's past fade, blending in with all the other houses.

Her mother must have been thinking along the same lines because she said, "I don't know what it is about this city. I swore I'd never live here again. But as soon as we separated, it was the only place I could think of to go."

Vanna remembered something she'd read about the city. "You know, it's named for Saint Anthony of Padua."

"Yeah."

"Do you know what he's the patron saint of?"

"What?"

Vanna put her hand on her mom's shoulder and said, "The lost."

30

"Grounded for three months," Alex said to Olivia. "That's harsh."

"You can't even talk on the phone," Vanna added, astonished.

Vanna had found her friends sitting on the floor in the back of the band hall. They moved to chairs as soon as Vanna pointed out that the section of carpet they were sitting on was the same spot where the low brass emptied their spit valves.

With football season almost over and all district band tryouts on the horizon, Mr. Mendez had given the band a free period. They were supposed to be working on their audition pieces, but for Vanna and her friends, discussing Olivia's punishment was much more interesting.

"I thought it would be worse," Fatima said. "Your mom's pretty tough."

"I know," Olivia said. "I was sure she'd ground me for the rest of my life, but she thinks I'm already too hard on myself. She doesn't want a perfect child. She wants a happy child and a safe child. That's why I got punished. I can't lie about where I am. It's dangerous."

"So if you're too hard on yourself, does that mean your mom won't expect you to be doing chores all the time and you can go out more?" Vanna asked.

"I don't know. We'll see. Rosa and I are supposed to divide up chores more evenly, which Rosa's not too happy about," Olivia said. "She helped me out, then ended up with a raw deal."

"Ah, chores aren't going to hurt that girl," Fatima said.

"Look who walked in," Alex said, then went back to playing with Fatima's fingers.

Olivia watched Travis sit down by Jake. She waited for her Travis paralysis to set in. It didn't. Instead, she had the overwhelming urge to talk to him again. So Olivia did something she never imagined she would ever do. She turned to Vanna and said, "Let's go talk to them."

Vanna's eyes widened slightly. "Okay."

Then plain old Olivia, without the special red dress or fancy hairstyle, approached Travis Martinez.

"Hey. Is he alive?" Olivia asked, pointing to Jake, who was sitting on the floor—earphones on and eyes closed.

"I'm not sure," Travis responded. "You get in trouble for being home late on Saturday?"

"I'm grounded for a while." She shrugged.

From there the conversation flowed easily. They talked about how strict their parents were and the newly formed peace between their sisters. Vanna stood back and let Olivia do all the talking.

The trumpet section leader reminded Travis that the trumpets were going to practice together, and he stood up to go join them. Their conversation was over, but Olivia didn't notice. Travis didn't seem to notice either. They stood there looking at each other for a few precious seconds.

Jake shattered the romantic moment by waking up and noticing Vanna. "Vanna, you should listen to Kings of Leon. They're country-influenced indie. You might like them since you're from up near Dallas and all."

EPILOGUE

One hot afternoon toward the end of April, Fatima, along with her brothers and sisters, squeezed into a crowded restaurant to celebrate Chula's first birthday. Getting her mother there had been a long process. It had started simply with phone calls, but it wasn't long before Lupe and her mother were seeing each other regularly. Lupe and Chula had even come over for Christmas. Mr. Garcia had refused to come to the party if "that boy" was going to be there. Fatima believed her dad would come around in time.

Luli bounced Chula and made shushing noises. Chula laughed.

"Lourdes, *ya*. Stop that," Mrs. Garcia snapped. "Give me the baby."

Luli handed Chula over. Chula began touching her grandmother's face.

"*Que chula mi Chula,*" Mrs. Garcia cooed.

"She likes you, *Mami,*" Lupe announced.

"Of course she does. She's a smart, smart girl." Mrs. Garcia and Chula babbled at each other as Lupe led them to a table where Ninfa was already sitting.

"*Ay! Que* pretty," Ninfa said. "Quick! I have to touch the baby before I give her *ojo.*" Ninfa squeezed Chula's cheeks, squealing, "Chula, Chula, Chula."

Fatima rolled her eyes at Lupe. The *ojo.* It had to be one of the weirdest superstitions. Supposedly, if you looked at something you wanted or someone you were jealous of, you could give "the evil eye." If you give something *ojo* and don't touch it, something bad could happen to it.

"Lupita, tell me you are not giving this baby soda," Mrs. Garcia said.

"No. I'm not a total *mensa,*" Lupe said. "She has her juice somewhere around here."

"When will she be baptized?"

"*Pues,* she's my daughter. I can—" Lupe started.

"Here," Fatima cut off her sister. She shoved the gift bags she had been carrying at Lupe.

Lupe opened the gifts from her family. They were a blanket her mother had crocheted and a picture book.

Ninfa handed Fatima a disposable camera. "I thought you might want this."

Fatima took a picture of her mother holding Chula. Later, she got some of Lupe blowing out the candle on Chula's cake, Chula smashing her fists into the cake, Chula

196

dunking her face in the cake, and Chula chewing on the book Fatima had given her.

Interacting with Eric and his family was awkward. Mrs. Garcia was polite, but Fatima could tell she was extremely uncomfortable. And who could blame her? Fatima wasn't sure how to feel about Eric either. She had liked him well enough before the whole pregnancy drama, and she supposed she would again. It would just take a little more time.

"We better go home. You need to get ready for that parade," Mrs. Garcia told Fatima as the party was winding down.

"Oh, yeah, the Flambeau Parade is tonight," Lupe said. "I'll look for you on TV, Fati."

"One more thing, Guadalupe." Mrs. Garcia reached into her purse, then pulled out an envelope that she pressed into Lupe's hand. "From your father and me."

Lupe opened the envelope and her eyes widened. Fatima could see there was money in it, but couldn't tell how much. "Mama, I . . ."

"Shh. For you to buy what you need for Chulita," Mrs. Garcia said. She kissed Lupe.

"Thank you, Mama," Lupe said. She hugged Fatima, and whispered, "And thanks, Fatima, for everything."

Olivia quickly changed out of her costume and left the dressing room. She had to hurry because Rosa was up next. It was Fiesta, a ten-day celebration of Texas's independence from Mexico. A busy time for everyone in San Antonio, especially marching bands and dancers. There were parades and festivals almost every day. Even though Olivia was taking only one dance class, her group had been performing all week.

Olivia squeezed into a spot between her mother and Travis. His sister was performing in the same show, and he was going to give Olivia a ride to school after Rosa performed. Even after all these months Olivia couldn't believe she and Travis were hanging out.

Rosa had planned a real showstopper full of complicated turns and rapid footwork. When the music stopped the audience roared. As another dance began, Travis whispered that they'd better leave.

Olivia kissed her mother goodbye, and they headed out of the Arneson Theatre.

Travis's car, a 1969 Mustang, must have been cool at one time, but now it was a rust-covered junker.

Travis opened the door for Olivia.

"You're going to have to roll down the window," he said as he got in the car. "The air-conditioning broke today. Once we get moving, it won't be so bad. I promise."

Olivia didn't buy that. Even a short drive in San Antonio without air-conditioning could be torture.

"Um, Travis, the window won't, uh, roll down," Olivia said. She had been turning the handle, but nothing was happening.

"Oh, yeah, it sometimes sticks on that side." He leaned

across her lap and began fiddling with the window. Olivia felt that familiar rush but was no longer nervous. Travis made her feel relaxed whenever they were together.

He banged on the door a bit and eventually the window slid down. He straightened up, turned on the car, and they were both blasted by reggaeton music.

"Sorry." He turned the dial until he found an oldies station.

"Horns up!" the drum major yelled. The band snapped their instruments into position as the drumline rattled off a cadence. Vanna counted four beats, then stepped with her left foot heel first. The woodwinds lowered their instruments as the trumpets played the opening measures of "Land of a Thousand Dances." The crowd roared as the band marched onto Broadway.

The air was charged with excitement. People packed the sides of the street. Old, young, all yelling, waving strings of neon lights or blowing plastic horns. Vanna was supposed to be looking straight ahead, but she couldn't stop staring at the crowd. Marching in the Flambeau Parade was a thousand times better than any football game.

Vanna had heard of Fiesta before she moved to San Antonio, but had never been in town for it. This year her mother decided they should experience all of it. Bob had come along a few times. He could be pretty dorky, but Vanna was getting used to him.

After "Land of a Thousand Dances," the band went into "The Hey Song." Vanna continued her crowd-watching while at the same time playing, staying in step, and keeping her row and line straight. She was looking for her father. He had promised he'd come. Since her birthday, she'd been good about calling him. She had even spent Christmas Day with him at her grandmother's. She'd been visiting her grandmother about once a week or so.

The band passed the section of seats the band boosters had reserved. Olivia and Fatima each had their families cheering for them. When the trombones passed them, Vanna heard Fatima's mother yell, "*Echale Banessa.*" Olivia's mother and Rosa yelled out her name, too. Then she spotted her mother and Bob cheering as loudly as everybody else. Mrs. Reynolds had turned out to be a pretty good band booster. She might not go to every meeting, but she came through on the important things.

A few blocks on, Vanna heard her name shouted again. Her father was shouting and waving madly from a hotel balcony. He had made it. Next to him was her grandmother. Vanna gave a small wave, so they would know she saw them.

"Fall in, freshman!" some section leader yelled.

The rest of the parade passed quickly. At the end, the band bolted for the air-conditioned buses. Inside, hats and jackets were quickly pulled off. The whole bus smelled of sweat and sunscreen. A few seniors huddled in the back of the bus, crying because they had just marched their last parade. Of course they had also cried on the way over to the parade because that had been their last bus ride to the Flambeau. Vanna hoped to God she didn't act like that when she became a senior.

Most of the seniors must have gotten on another bus to cry because there were plenty of seats on Vanna's bus. Vanna and Olivia had their own seats. Even their instruments had a seat. Fatima and Alex snuck onto their bus and shared a seat. Alex sat with his back against the window, and Fatima sat leaning against his chest. They looked comfortable together.

Jake stretched out on the seat behind Vanna. He wasn't her boyfriend, but he was her friend. She wanted to get to know him really well before possibly taking things to the next level.

The bus driver had turned on some Tejano music, which elicited a groan from Jake. Selena's "Como La Flor" came on. Fatima had translated it for Vanna. It was about wishing someone well when he finds love with someone else. That was the attitude Vanna tried to have with Caitlyn and Troy. It didn't hurt to think about Troy anymore. In fact, Vanna rarely thought of him at all.

Vanna watched San Antonio pass by. The city looked very different from the subdivisions of matching brick houses and clean paved streets she'd grown up around. In San Antonio, there were houses painted random bright colors: pinks, purples, oranges, greens. Nothing matched. Huge statues of the Virgin Mary seemed to be the lawn art of choice, and people still had their Christmas lights up in April.

So it wasn't Plano. She wasn't the same girl she had been in Plano. Maybe she didn't go to as many parties or live in as big a house. She had better friends than she'd ever had in Plano, and she and her mother had never been closer.

Maybe this city loved its Alamo a little too much, but the Alamo and the river were growing on her, too. She ate at the Alamo Café, bought her sheet music at Alamo Music, shopped at the Alamo Quarry Market, and had even called Alamo Plumbing Repair.

"If you could live anywhere in the world, where would you live?" Vanna asked her two best friends.

"I'd like to say someplace exciting like New York, but it gets too cold there," Fatima said.

"How about Mexico City?" Alex interjected. "Pretty warm there."

"Earthquakes," Fatima answered.

"Too scary," Olivia said.

"Where would you live?" Vanna asked Olivia.

"I kind of like where I am now."

"Me, too," Vanna said. "I really like where I am." And she meant it.